TORY TOP ROAD
BRANCH

THE
TIFFIN

D0317161

THE TIFFIN

MAHTAB NARSIMHAN

HOT
KEY
BOOKS

Originally published in Canada by Cormorant Books Inc., Toronto, 2011

This edition published in Great Britain in 2014 by Hot Key Books
Northburgh House, 10 Northburgh Street, London EC1V 0AT

Copyright © Mahtab Narsimhan 2011
Illustration copyright © Jet Purdie 2014

The moral rights of the author have been asserted.

All rights reserved.
No part of this publication may be reproduced, stored or transmitted
in any form by any means, electronic, mechanical, photocopying or
otherwise, without the prior written permission of the publisher.

All characters in this publication are fictitious and any resemblance to real
persons, living or dead, is purely coincidental.

A CIP catalogue record for this book is available from the British Library.

ISBN: 978-1-4714-0292-0

1

This book is typeset in 11pt Sabon using Atomik ePublisher

Printed and bound by Clays Ltd, St Ives Plc

FSC

Hot Key Books supports the Forest Stewardship Council (FSC),
the leading international forest certification organisation, and is
committed to printing only on Greenpeace-approved FSC-certified paper.

www.hotkeybooks.com

Hot Key Books is part of the Bonnier Publishing Group
www.bonnierpublishing.com

For Pervin Mehrotra

Author's Note

The tiffin delivery service is a hundred and fifty years old, and available only in the vibrant city of Bombay (Mumbai), India. The *dabbawallas* deliver home-cooked food to the thousands of white-collar workers who subscribe to this service, and return the empty tiffins to their homes after the meal has been eaten. These semi-literate tiffin carriers employ a primitive alpha-numeric code for tracking, and, using every manner of local transport available, deliver the hot food on time, every day. They have an enviable track record — only one box in six million is lost.

Chapter One

April 1982
My dearest A,
I'm so scared! You have to meet me tonight ...
Anahita stared at the note. The letters glared back at her. She imagined Anurag reading it, trying to absorb the news. His green eyes would widen, he'd take a deep breath, exhale. She could imagine every emotion that would play out on his handsome face. What would he do next? Call her? Come running over? Or would he ignore the note?

The shrill doorbell jerked her out of her reverie.

"Young *memsahib*, are the tiffins ready?" a man called out. She heard every word clearly through the thin wooden door of their flat.

Anahita folded the note with trembling hands, put it into a bit of plastic, and tucked it between two warm *chapatis* in the first of the tiffin's three compartments. The other two had already been filled; one with *dal* and the other with spicy cauliflower-potatoes. She slid the tiffin into its cylindrical aluminum case carefully, and snapped the clasp to lock it.

"Coming," she called out. She grabbed three more tiffins

1

from the kitchen counter and hurried to the door with her heavy load. Her mother was praying in the living room, swaying from side to side as she recited the words softly. She glanced up as Anahita passed by, then frowned and waved her on, her lips continuing to move in prayer.

"I'm leaving," the nasal voice continued. "The trains don't wait for anyone."

"*Coming*," said Anahita, louder this time, stoking her anger. If she was angry enough, there would be no room for the fear that gripped her heart.

Anahita placed the tiffins on the floor and flung open the door, ready to give the *dabbawalla* an earful. A scrawny vulture of a man stood there, pulling at his beaked nose.

"Who are you? Where is Amit?"

The sweaty *dabbawalla* wiped his face with a filthy red rag, flicked off his Gandhi cap, slapped it against his thigh, and set it back on his head at a jaunty angle.

"Amit is sick. I am his substitute and almost late," he said. He had the air of a man who had repeated his story many times already. He held out a grimy hand for the tiffins.

Anahita passed them over — all except one, which she clutched to her chest. This wasn't just food, it was her future. And she was about to hand it over to a stranger. Of all days, why did her regular *dabbawalla* have to be sick today? Was this a sign?

"How do I know you won't run away with my tiffins?" she whispered, struggling to keep her voice steady.

The man sighed and stepped aside. Behind him on the landing lit by the harsh white of a tube light, a long

2

rectangular wooden carrier cradled fifteen tiffins. Anahita glanced at the familiar aluminum cases with colourful letters and numbers on their lids, some in so shaky a hand it seemed as if a person with fever had painted them.

"Young *memsahib*, an empty tiffin box costs ten rupees in the market. With the food, it's worth maybe fifteen rupees. Do you think I could retire after I steal it?" the man said. "I'm getting late. Do you want your husband to get his lunch or not? That last one's for him, isn't it?" He jerked his chin at the tiffin Anahita was still hugging.

Husband. Anahita repeated the alien word to herself silently, savouring its taste on her tongue. She handed over the tiffin with a trembling hand.

"Are you okay?" he said in a softer voice. "You look ill."

Bile rose in her throat. Anahita glanced behind her furtively. "I'm fine," she said. "You're sure this will reach Anurag Parekh? At Mittal Towers, Nariman Point, eleventh floor? You won't lose it, will you? Because you see he ... er ... has a weak stomach. He can't eat any other food. He must get this tiffin."

She knew she was babbling. The man raised his hand to stop her.

"Young *memsahib*, this tiffin has reached your husband every day, no? Why should today be any different? Anyway, the address is right here," he said, tapping the lid of the tiffin, "and it will reach him no matter who delivers it. Besides, I have never lost a box."

"Shhhh, you don't have to raise your voice," said Anahita. "I'm not deaf." She stole another quick glance behind her.

3

The hallway was still deserted but she knew it wouldn't be for much longer. The moment the prayers were finished, her mother would be eavesdropping. She turned back to the *dabbawalla* and stared at him. "Are you telling me the truth? You've never lost a tiffin?"

The *dabbawalla* dropped his gaze. "Well, just one — a long time ago," he said. He looked up again. "But I won't lose yours. Your husband will get the tiffin. He will come home a happy man in the evening. Trust me."

Anahita took a deep breath. Yes, let him come tonight. Please. He has to! She imagined the look on her mother's face, the disappointment in her father's eyes. She couldn't face it all by herself. She needed Anurag's support.

The *dabbawalla* arranged the tiffins in the carrier, chattering away. Anahita watched her precious missive nestle among the others, snug and comfortable. Safe.

He hoisted the carrier onto his head with a grunt. A cloud of foul-smelling body odour wafted her way. Anahita clapped her hand to her mouth and backed away, the urge to vomit overpowering. She took deep breaths and the feeling subsided.

The man descended the gloomy staircase, carrying her tiffin further away with each step. Anahita had a mad urge to run and snatch it back. She still had a chance. Once the *dabbawalla* merged into the river of people on the street, there would be no recalling the note. Should she call Anurag instead? But that would mean using the public phone booth and having to endure the questioning looks of the neighbours and vendors who knew her.

Suddenly, she wasn't sure she had done the right thing. Not sure at all. Blood pounded in her ears and her legs trembled. She had to retrieve the note. This was a huge mistake!

Anahita hurried towards the stairs. A shuffling of feet arrested her steps. Her mother stood by the door, questions written all over her face. Too late. Anahita pushed past her mother and raced to the window just in time to see the *dabbawalla* turn the corner of their lane and vanish from sight. She closed her eyes, clasped the pendant of Ahura Mazda in her clammy hands, and recited an *Ashem Vohu*, feeling her mother's eyes burning holes into her back.

Andheri station seethed with people. In a corner of the platform, a group of men in white *dhoti-kurtas* and Gandhi caps waded through a sea of tiffins, sorting them at top speed. There was no shade at that end of the station and the sun beat down fiercely, heating up the tiffins, as well as the tempers of the *dabbawallas*. Sporadic bickering broke out among them.

The leader, Vinayak, distinguished only by a red band around his right arm, shaded his eyes and peered down the length of the platform.

"Where is that replacement of Amit's?" he said. "He should have been here by now!" He spat out a mouthful of betel-nut juice onto the train tracks, narrowly missing a passerby on the platform. "I hate it when a team member is not on time!"

"He's new to this route, Vinayak," one of the men replied. "He may be a bit slower in collecting the tiffins.

Plus, you know what the housewives are like when they see a substitute. They will ask ten questions before handing over their tiffins — as if they contain gold." He rolled his eyes and a couple of *dabbawallas* laughed.

The plaintive cry of a train's horn sounded in the distance. The ten a.m. to Churchgate was arriving.

Vinayak cursed under his breath and paced. If that idiot of a substitute was late, he would ruin the timing of so many others. The *dabbawallas* prided themselves on being punctual. Always. The tiffins had to be delivered by twelve sharp to their customers spread all over Bombay. No one ever went hungry because of a lost or delayed box.

"There he is," someone shouted. Vinayak saw a battered tiffin carrier sailing towards them at top speed, high above the heads of the throng. Behind them the train chugged into the station. A whiff of unwashed bodies and rusting metal filled the air.

"Come on," yelled Vinayak. "Move or we'll all miss the train!"

Amit's replacement, panting and dripping with sweat, flapped towards them with an ungainly gait. Four pairs of arms slid the carrier to the ground and, with machine-like precision, started sorting. Until the tiffins were further sorted according to final destination, none of the carriers could be loaded on the train. People were already climbing aboard, blocking the entrance.

"*Jaldi*," said Vinayak, urging them on. His team members' hands were blurs as they obeyed him. The metal tiffin cases clanged against each other, adding to the cacophony.

Within seconds the sorting was done. The sound of the horn pierced the air again and the train started moving. Four *dabbawallas* ran alongside and slid their carriers into separate compartments, onto the toes of commuters who crowded the open doors. A volley of yells and curses fell on deaf ears as the men jumped in. The train clattered over the steel tracks, settling into its familiar staccato rhythm.

Already exhausted from the sprint to the station, Amit's replacement was the last to get on. He slid the heavy carrier into a compartment. Something blocked its way and half the carrier still hung out. The train gathered speed. He jogged alongside, trying to shove the carrier inside.

"Get in and pull, you moron!" Vinayak yelled out to the *dabbawalla*'s receding back. The crowds moved in and Vinayak lost sight of him.

The compartment had almost reached the edge of the platform when the *dabbawalla* managed to jump on board. He pushed the passengers aside and dragged the carrier in just as they passed a telephone pole. A corner of the carrier slammed against the pole with a resounding crack.

A tiffin at the very end leaped into the air, somersaulted towards the glistening steel tracks, and rolled to a standstill on a wooden sleeper.

Chapter Two

Thirteen years later

Kunal opened the first of the tiffin's compartments. Coal-black eyes stared at him — they were vaguely familiar. He set the box aside with trembling hands and peered into the second compartment. From the depths of the watery dal, a dozen eyeballs floated to the surface. They were all fixed on him, and glaring menacingly. Suddenly, he knew exactly whom they belonged to: Badri.

With a shriek, he flung the box away and jerked awake, his heart racing.

Thunder rolled across the sky. A jagged scar of lightning lit up his room. It was empty.

Kunal was bathed in sweat, yet unbelievably cold. This was the worst nightmare he had ever had! And it was all thanks to the new cook, Badri.

Within seconds Sethji was at the door, his face lit up with anger in the intermittent flashes of lightning.

"Who just screamed and ruined my sleep?" said Sethji.

"Was that you?"

Kunal could still see those floating eyeballs, all of them fixed on him. He hugged the threadbare sheet tighter around him, even though the heat was stifling.

"Don't just sit there like an idiot," bellowed Sethji. "Answer me!"

"I-I had a bad dream," said Kunal, when he could find his voice. "It was horrible."

"What?" roared Sethji, drowning out a roll of thunder. "For that you shriek like a girl and wake us all up? You're nothing but a sissy."

Mrs. Seth peeked out from behind Sethji's ample frame, but said nothing.

"I'm sorry," said Kunal, his voice catching in his throat. *I will not cry, I will not cry*, he repeated to himself fiercely, over and over again. "I've been having the same dream these past few nights, and it's all because of Badri. I don't like him. He's been acting creepy lately and staring, always staring at me. Only me," he finished in a whisper. A flash of lightning illuminated Sethji's face. Was it shock that Kunal saw? Pity? Fear even? Was it possible that Sethji believed him? The very next moment he had the answer.

"Shut up, you liar!" said Sethji. "You've had a bad attitude towards Badri ever since we hired him two months ago and now you're telling stories to get him into trouble? He's my friend and he's doing me a favour by staying on to cook. Any five-star hotel would have hired him like that." Sethji snapped his pudgy fingers. A soft, whooshy sound was all he could produce. "I'm not buying this *faltu-giri*. NOT AT

9

ALL! He's probably watching you because you're lazy and a work-shirker. And I'll encourage him to keep at it."

Kunal's eyes strayed to Mrs. Seth's white face. She knew he was telling the truth. *Say something*, he beseeched her silently. But she did nothing.

Sethji advanced on Kunal, wearing his usual expression; a combination of contempt and anger. "What really happened? The truth now. You're aware of the consequences of lying to me."

Kunal nodded. He knew them only too well. And he knew Sethji, too, who did not like anything disrupting his carefully arranged world. Especially an inconvenient truth.

"I fell off the bed in my sleep and so I yelled," said Kunal, in a flat voice

"That's better," said Sethji. "Are you hurt?"

Kunal shook his head. "Pity," said Sethji, still glaring at him.

"At least leave him alone at night," said Mrs. Seth, in a strangled voice. "Come back to bed. We have to get up in a couple of hours, anyway." Her fingers fluttered up and down her thin plait.

"You wake me up once more and you'll regret it," snarled Sethji. He shoved Kunal, who staggered backward. "And the next time you feel the need to scream like a girl, stuff a pillow in your mouth or I'll do it for you."

Kunal stared at those piggy eyes that shone blackly in the flashes of lightning and wished he could poke something into them. Sethji plodded back to his room behind Mrs. Seth, muttering to himself. Another drum roll of thunder reverberated from one end of the sky to the other.

It matched the thunderstorm raging in Kunal's chest. Sleep was out of the question. He could not risk that nightmare again. He groped under the mattress and his hand closed over something smooth and cool. He drew it out, clutched it to his chest and padded over to the window.

Kunal stood there, his thoughts as dark as the night outside. Sethji knew Kunal was right about Badri but would never admit it. Sethji needed a cook more than he needed a waiter and Kunal knew he would just have to endure the unfairness. But for a moment there it almost seemed like Sethji had believed him.

The skies opened up and rain came hurtling down. Kunal pressed his forehead against the cold metal bars on the window, angry at allowing himself to think this way, to have the slightest hope. He was on his own and had been since the day he was born; an orphan the Seths had adopted, and now a slave who was fed scraps and made to work without wages. He gripped the glass bangle, his mother's last possession, given to him by Mrs. Seth, held it tighter and wished she were here, with him. Wished he could lead the life of a normal boy with homework the only worry on his mind.

Kunal had no idea how long he stood by the window, staring at the deserted road and the dark windows in the buildings opposite, his mind churning with the possibility of escape. It was only when he heard Sethji clump downstairs that he knew another miserable day had begun and he was already exhausted.

11

Mrs. Seth banged on his door. "I want you downstairs in the next ten minutes." And then she was gone. Kunal stared at the rain beyond his window. The whole world was melting. The relentless downpour seemed to have washed away all colour, leaving it bleak and grey. He gazed at a tiny scrap of red cloth on a TV antenna in the distance — a smear of colour in the bland landscape. He had to tilt his head sideways to see it, past a jutting roof. Though sodden with rain, it fluttered each time a breath of wind flitted past.

"Kunal! Come down now!" Mrs. Seth called out from halfway up the stairs. "I know you're awake."

He stood up, feeling his heartbeat quicken. He turned to go, his eyes still riveted to that brave scrap of red.

"Coming!" he said.

"Are your legs broken?" she called out again. "Can't you move any faster? You think the customers will serve themselves?"

Kunal returned the bangle to its hiding place under the mattress and slipped out of his room, which was barely larger than a closet, closing the door behind him. Its rusty hinges squeaked in protest. There was a hole where the lock should have been. Sethji had removed it years ago. When Kunal had asked about replacing it, Sethji had laughed and said beggars did not need privacy. He should consider himself lucky he had a roof over his head and three meals a day. Kunal had never asked again.

He padded downstairs noiselessly, but there was no need. It was like descending into a whirlpool of chaos, even though it was only seven in the morning.

12

Sethji was yelling at Kunal's fellow waiter and friend, Lalan, who towered over the proprietor and yet listened to the admonishments meekly. Their eyes met and Lalan winked, earning a parting whack from Sethji. Fans whirred noisily, churning up the humid air in the dining room along with dust, flies, dirt, and despair, and hurling it over the dozen or so sweaty heads of the breakfasting customers. There would be at least twice that amount at peak time, but for now, the cramped and grimy room was relatively empty.

Mrs. Seth frowned at him from the foot of the stairs.

"Why are you looking like a two-day-old *chapati*?" she said. "Look lively." She slapped the back of his head with a bony hand. His brains scuttled to the front.

"I have a bad feeling about Badri," said Kunal, searching her face. "There is something very wrong with him, like I told Sethji last night. Badri always asks me to stay back late to help clean the kitchen. And while I clean he watches me. Don't you find that odd?"

Mrs. Seth, all jagged lines and sharp corners, stared at him. "What rubbish! Don't let Sethji hear you say that again."

"But it's true and you know it," said Kunal. "Why won't you believe me?"

"Badri is a friend of Sethji's and you're an orphan. Who do you think we're going to believe?"

"Me, of course!" he said, and meant it.

"Don't give me any cheek early in the morning," said Mrs. Seth, vinegar in her voice. Yet her eyes were soft, almost as if she were in pain. "Sethji is very upset about being woken up last night. You'd better not give him any more reason

13

to be cranky. You know what's in store for all you waiters when that happens."

"But really, Mrs. Seth, I'm telling the truth —"

"Enough," she said. She glanced at some customers who had just walked in and were settling themselves at empty tables. "Vinayak has brought the empty tiffins. Take them to Badri and be quick. It's starting to get busy."

Kunal's stomach clenched. He walked to the entrance of the *dhaba* where the neatly lined-up tiffin cases glistened with rain. Grabbing a couple in each hand, he picked his way between the tables and scurrying waiters and headed towards the kitchen. He hesitated just outside the door, his heart thudding, hoping Badri was so busy he would not have time to stop and stare. Kunal took a deep breath and pushed through the swinging doors.

Badri dominated the tiny, food-splattered kitchen, moving nimbly between four large gas burners. Steam from huge pots of goat curry, *sambar*, and boiled rice wafted up and mingled into a fragrant cloud, almost obscuring the skinny cook, who was clad only in ragged shorts.

"Kunal, my friend, how are you this morning?" said Badri with a smile. Though his tone was casual, he was ogling in earnest.

"I'm all right," Kunal mumbled. Around them kitchen helpers scurried to and fro, chopping, cutting, stirring, but Badri did not spare them a single glance. He had eyes only for Kunal.

"I'll save you some of my special goat curry for lunch," said Badri. "I like to look after my friends." He inched a

14

little closer and winked. Kunal took a step back.

"Thanks," said Kunal, "but that's all right." He almost threw the tiffins in a corner and ran out to get the rest. Standing so close to Badri made him uneasy. Even more than his creepy looks and his devious ways to be alone with Kunal as often as possible.

In the narrow passage connecting the kitchen and dining room, Kunal stopped for a moment and took deep breaths. This was getting unbearable. Even in the day he could not escape those eyes, those lewd looks! Another waiter and Sethji's pet, Raju, deliberately bumped into him, shoving him against the damp wall. Kunal glared at him, rubbing his scraped elbow.

"Hey, pretty boy," Raju said. "Why don't you watch where you're going? Or are those green eyes made of glass?"

"Why don't *you* watch it?" muttered Kunal as he wrestled to keep his temper under control.

"For a nobody, you're acting pretty smart," said Raju. "One day I'll teach you a lesson you badly need."

Kunal should have been used to the taunts about his good looks by now, but he still felt like punching that smirking face. Just then Lalan ambled past with an armful of dirty dishes. Kunal pressed himself against the wall to make room. Raju stood his ground.

"What's the matter?" said Lalan, leaning towards Raju, crowding him. "Did I miss something?"

Raju took a step back, his face pale as he stared up at Lalan. "N-nothing."

"If you bother Kunal again you'll have me to answer

to," said Lalan. His calm expression belied the menace in his voice.

Raju ran towards the dining room.

"You'd better tell your friends, too," Lalan called out. "This is the last warning."

The waiter shot through the swinging doors without looking back.

"Thanks, *yaar!*" said Kunal. "I don't know what I'd do without you."

Lalan winked and headed to the kitchen. Kunal continued on to the dining room.

Once all the tiffins were in the kitchen, he helped with serving breakfast to the masses of blue-collar workers who stopped by Bombay Bahar to gossip and fill their stomachs with greasy food before starting another day of drudgery. Kunal approached the fly-infested counter for the next pickup.

"*Chai* and *anda bhurji* for Vinayak are ready," hollered the kitchen helper.

"I'll take it," said Kunal, lunging for the counter, a few steps ahead of another waiter.

Kunal grabbed the tea and scrambled eggs cooked in butter, onions, chilies, tomatoes, and sweat — and worked his way to Vinayak, who sat at a table in a corner of the room. The *dabbawalla*, a regular at the *dhaba*, had an open newspaper in front of him. His shrewd eyes, which normally missed nothing, were glazed and vacant today. As always, something tugged at Kunal's heart whenever he saw this old man. He'd heard rumours that Vinayak had had a "major tragedy" in his life, but Kunal did not know what the tragedy was, and had not had the courage to ask him about it yet. The *dabbawalla* had been coming to the *dhaba* for just over four years, and yet Kunal felt he'd known him all his life and looked forward to seeing the familiar face every weekday morning.

Kunal placed the food on the wobbly Formica tabletop. "Good morning, Vinayakji," he said, addressing the older man respectfully.

Vinayak snapped out of his trance and looked up at Kunal. His eyes were tinged with red, as if he hadn't slept all night. "How are you, my friend?"

"Okay," said Kunal. "Is everything all right? You looked so sad a moment ago. Anything bothering you?"

"Just tired," said Vinayak. He leaned back in his chair and glanced around him. "But thank you for asking."

"You've helped me so much, Vinayakji," said Kunal. "If there's anything a lowly waiter can do ..."

Vinayak shook his head and smiled. Kunal loved the way his eyes crinkled up at the corners. "I'll keep it in mind. And who are you calling a lowly waiter? You're a very good one!"

"I'd rather be a *dabbawalla*," said Kunal. "It must be such fun. Being a waiter in this *dhaba* is really ... you know ...," he lowered his voice and took a quick look around, "*painful*!"

Another bedraggled smile traipsed across Vinayak's face as he shook his head. "Drums always sound better from a distance."

Kunal frowned. "Meaning?"

"Every job has its good and bad points," replied Vinayak.

"Ever tried to wade through flood waters up to your chest to do your job?"

Kunal shook his head.

"Ever had to navigate the roads during a strike?"

"No, Vinayakji," said Kunal, gazing at the older man's face, which was a railway map of lines.

"Well then, my friend, you're better off here at the *dhaba*."

"No!" said Kunal. It burst out of him a bit louder than he intended. A few heads turned in his direction.

"Oi, stupid, there are other people waiting to be served!" yelled Sethji. "Stop chit-chatting and get on with your work."

"That's for me," said Kunal. "And I think you should know: I don't plan on staying here too long. I hate it here."

Vinayak smiled again, a nice warm smile this time. "You'd better go now. We'll talk some more tomorrow. Don't make any hasty decisions."

Kunal nodded and dashed back to the counter. He grabbed another order of tea and fried eggs and picked his way over to table number six.

"Your mother must have been one good-looking woman. Look what she produced," someone hissed behind him. "*Kasam se*, I'd love to meet her!"

Kunal's hand shook violently and hot tea scalded his skin. The plate of eggs crashed to the floor, yolks oozing yellow over shards of white china.

Kunal whipped around to face a hulk of a man who sat at table five, calmly eating a *paratha*. He slammed the glass of tea on the table and glared at the man. "How dare you speak about my mother like that. Take it back."

"*Jhootha!*" said the hulk, not meeting Kunal's eye. "I didn't say anything. Now get lost and clear this mess before you go." It was obvious he had not expected Kunal to answer back.

Kunal stared at him, a helpless rage bubbling up inside. Recklessness, too. "Obviously, you mustn't have had a mother or you wouldn't be talking this way. You were probably found in the gutter," he said, loud enough for the entire *dhaba* to hear.

There was pin-drop silence. He had everyone's undivided attention.

"You worthless insect," said the hulk. "You stand there and insult me? Me? The one who puts food in your mouth?"

"What is going on, boy?" said Sethji, waddling up to them. He whacked Kunal on the back of his head. "Breaking my expensive plates again, I see."

"This gorilla insulted me and my mother and made me drop the plate. Honest!" said Kunal.

"Seth, if you make it a habit of employing liars in your *dhaba*, I'll stop eating here and tell all my friends, too," said the hulk. "You're going to lose a lot of business."

Sethji paled. "Calm down," he said. Then he turned to Kunal, his eyes murderous. "Don't blame your butterfingers on our paying customers. You're a liar — it runs in your blood. Apologize before I give you a thrashing you'll never forget!"

Kunal quailed at the expression on Sethji's face. The *dhaba* was Sethji's life and money was his God. Any harm to either and Sethji would be more dangerous than a rabid dog. And yet Kunal could not get himself to apologize.

"Seth, this is ridiculous," said Vinayak, who had appeared in their midst. "I know Kunal. He does not lie. This idiot must have started it."

Kunal glanced at Vinayak gratefully. Whenever Sethji tried to bully him, the *dabbawalla* always stood up for Kunal. If only Sethji could have treated him with a little bit of respect rather than a slave he would have said he was sorry. But not now — not when he was being humiliated and it hurt!

"Who the hell d'you think you are?" said the hulk. "Sethji, why is this old goat butting in?"

"I'll thank you to keep your long nose out of this," snapped Sethji, glaring at Vinayak. "Go back to your table."

"There are two sides to every story and everyone deserves respect, even your waiters," said Vinayak in a cold voice. "If you don't handle this fairly, I'll have to talk to the Dabbawalla Association about finding another supplier for our customers' tiffins. Someone more humane."

Sethji's eyes darted from the hulk to Vinayak. Sweat beaded his forehead. For a moment, no one spoke.

"Why is everyone standing around when there is work to be done?" said Mrs. Seth as she walked up to them briskly. "I'll handle this."

Vinayak nodded and ambled back to his table. Sethji, visibly relieved, walked away to his perch behind the cash register. Mrs. Seth turned to face the hulk and stared up at him without flinching.

"No one mistreats our boys but us," she said. "Don't think I can't tell the Truckers' Union a thing or two about you. I wonder how long you'll remain employed after that."

The hulk mumbled a curse and sat down as raucous laughter rippled through the packed dining room.

"Shut up!" he said. He thumped a fist on the table and glared at everyone. There was immediate silence.

"As for you," Mrs. Seth said, turning to Kunal, "get back to work. You've caused enough trouble for one day."

Kunal started to walk away when Mrs. Seth hauled him back roughly. *Now what?* he thought.

"Stupid boy!" she hissed. "Watch out for the glass."

Kunal realized he had been about to step on the shards with bare feet. "Thank you!"

"Don't thank me," she snapped. "You think I'm going to pay for a doctor if you cut your foot? Clean this mess up immediately." She marched back to the kitchen.

Kunal picked up the broken china and stood up. The hulk stuck his foot out and Kunal had no choice but to stop. His pulse raced as he looked into the trucker's cold, black eyes. "Make me a laughing stock, will you?" he whispered. "I'll get you, smart boy. Out there, when you least expect it. We'll see who has the last laugh."

Kunal managed to walk back to the kitchen on shaky legs. He stayed there, feeling Badri's eyes bore holes into his back, until the hulk left.

Chapter Three

Kunal waited impatiently as Badri filled up all the tiffin boxes with his concoctions, which varied on a daily basis. Today it was goat curry in the bottom box, masala eggplant with a dab of mango pickle in the middle one, and a dollop of rice with two *chapatis* in the topmost box. The kitchen helper cleaned the spills on the outside of the tiffins, slid them into their aluminum carriers, and snapped the clasps shut. Soon the tiffins were ready to make their journey to the station, and onward to the city centre.

As Vinayak had explained to Kunal, they would change many hands before reaching their owners, sharp at noon. Two hundred thousand boxes would be delivered in this precise way, each and every day of the week. In three hours the *dabbawallas* would cover an area of almost forty miles, then make the reverse journey to bring the boxes back.

Kunal brought the heavy tiffins to the entrance two at a time. Vinayak was waiting by the door, his Gandhi cap covering a black mop of hair shot through with silver. The plastic cape thrown over his shoulders was really just a large garbage bag slit along one side. It was still pouring and the pavement was slick and shiny. A slow-moving river of umbrellas bobbed past. Water gushed noisily into the gutter. The honking of traffic was steadily growing louder. Vinayak arranged the tiffins within the carrier.

"Can I help you sort them?" asked Kunal. "Will you show me how?" He had asked this question often in the past but Vinayak had always been in a hurry to get to the station as soon as the tiffins were filled. He looked at the old man hopefully.

Vinayak glanced at his watch, then back at Kunal, an unfathomable expression in his eyes. "All right." He picked up one rain-shiny box and moved closer to Kunal.

"This number-letter combination at the bottom is the most important part; it's the destination station, building, and floor. So '9 AI 12' means this tiffin is to be delivered to the twelfth floor of the Air India Building at Nariman Point, which is area code nine. The number three in the centre means this has to go to Churchgate. Clear so far?"

Kunal nodded. "And the letters VLP and E?"

"I see you've been practising your reading," said Vinayak. "Very good! I'm glad my efforts were not wasted."

Kunal grinned. "Never! I love learning."

Vinayak patted him on the back. "That is the originating address of the tiffin," he continued. "We have to make sure the tiffin gets back too, right? So VLP is Vile Parle and the E stands for Hanuman Road within that area. Lesson over for today. I had better get going."

"You didn't tell me about the red circle," said Kunal.

Vinayak laughed. "Looks like you're planning to deliver

a tiffin right now. It's for easy identification at Churchgate when the teams have to pick up their boxes for deliveries. They're all colour-coded. Simple, isn't it?"

"Yes," said Kunal. "I think I could learn this quite easily."

Vinayak ruffled his hair with a wet hand. "An intelligent boy like you? Of course you could, Kunal, but now I must run or I'll miss the train. They're our lifeline. And if we're late, our customers have to wait, or go hungry. No *dabbawalla* can afford to let that happen."

"Thank you for speaking up for me," said Kunal. "Only Lalan here will."

Vinayak stared at him for a long moment from under the plastic cape. Water dripped from the tip of his nose but he barely noticed it. The rain came down harder, beating on the aluminum tiffins that lay between them, splashing onto his bare toes. Kunal wished he could climb into the carrier and be whisked away by Vinayak, never to return.

"This happens often, does it not?" said Vinayak.

Kunal thought of all the instances when Sethji had humiliated him, yelled at him in front of a roomful of customers. Sethji never once treated him with kindness. He blinked furiously to keep from crying.

"If things ever get too bad here, you come to me. Okay?"

"You really mean that?" asked Kunal. He searched Vinayak's face. Was he serious? In all the years he had known Vinayak, this was the first time he had made such an offer.

"Yes," said the *dabbawalla*.

"But how will I know where to find you?"

"I live in the *chawl* at 51, Janpath Lane. I'm on the third

24

floor, room number five."

Kunal frowned, trying to memorize the address. From the corner of his eye, he noticed Sethji glaring at him and tapping his watch.

"I have to go," said Kunal.

"Here, I'll write it down for you," said Vinayak. He ducked into the *dhaba* and quickly scribbled the address on a page of his small notebook, tore it out and gave it to Kunal. "It's not too far from here. If you ran, you'd get to me within ten minutes."

"Thank you," said Kunal. He tucked the note into his pocket and watched Vinayak hoist the carrier on to his head with an expertise that spoke of years of practice. With a little nod, Vinayak loped away, the black garbage bag flapping behind him.

The rest of the day went by in a blur of heat, food, and flies. A tide of people surged and ebbed through Bombay Bahar. Kunal ate a meal of watery *dal*, rice, and mutton bones with the other waiters standing in the kitchen during a brief lull. The food seemed to sink straight to his feet and leak away, leaving him no more than a shell of skin and bone. There wasn't enough food for a second helping, or enough time, either. And he was definitely not accepting any food from Badri, no matter how starved he was.

The next wave of hungry customers descended and Kunal was at their table, polishing the Formica with a greasy rag and taking their order.

At five in the evening, he got a break for a couple of

hours. A new shift of boys poured in. The first batch was off. Some went home or to other jobs. For Kunal there was no escape. He had to report back downstairs at seven o'clock. He hobbled up to his room, lay down on the bed, and fell asleep almost instantly. But not before he extracted the green glass bangle that had once belonged to his mother, run his fingers over its smooth surface for the millionth time, and tucked it away safely under the mattress, out of reach of Sethji's grubby hands.

A fair woman with green eyes stood in front of him. An angel ... surely his mother. She was so beautiful that Kunal could barely look at her. His heart ached with pride and joy. She opened her arms wide and called out to him ... "KUNAL!"

The word exploded in his dreams and jarred him awake. He sat up, heart pounding, and glanced out the window. Darkness had softened the shabby appearance of the houses opposite. Here and there the soft glow of a lamp shone through. In other windows the harsh, unforgiving glare of a tube light spilled out. Rain still pattered on his windowsill, mixed with the sounds of the traffic and the buzz of chatter from the *dhaba* below. He got out of bed and switched on the light. On the walls around him were damp patches in grotesque shapes. Sometimes he would lie there and stare at the watermarks; he'd see a dog with its teeth bared, or a pair of splayed hands reaching out to strangle him, or a spider, waiting to pounce. Today the walls just wept.

"Don't make me come up!"

They're really missing me, thought Kunal as he splashed

his face in the tiny bathroom just outside his room. He ran a damp hand through his hair, brushed his teeth with his finger, and was ready to face the world.

He walked downstairs and his eyes went straight to the clock. Seven-thirty. He was in trouble.

"Why can't you be on time?" Mrs. Seth said as soon as she saw him. "Don't you know better by now?"

"Sorry," mumbled Kunal.

"Go serve table ten, and for God's sake, stay out of trouble," she said. Their eyes met and he glimpsed something there ... but it was gone in an instant. Mrs. Seth hurried into the kitchen, wiping her sweaty face with her *dupatta*.

Kunal went straight to the pickup counter covered with plates of food, each crowned with a halo of flies. Under each plate was a chit with a table number. He found the number ten, barely visible because of the orange oil saturating the paper, and hurried with the steaming plate of *sambar* and rice to a scruffy customer scratching his long hair, flecked with dandruff.

"If this food is as tasty as you look ...," the man said, leering at Kunal.

Kunal ignored him, plunked the food on the table and sidled along the periphery of the room back to the counter. It was a roundabout route, but a lot safer in the evening when some of the more rowdy customers came in. Most of them would have imbibed the cheap alcohol from the bootleg liquor bars that abounded in the area and would be bolder, touching or pinching him at every opportunity.

"Kunal," Sethji called out. "Over here!"

Kunal walked up to him, flinching a bit, and hating himself for it.

"Delivery. New customer at Pandit Road. Here's the address," said Sethji. "Be quick."

Kunal's heart raced. Freedom for a short while. And he knew exactly which route he was going to take on the way home, after the delivery. He lowered his eyes, afraid the excitement would show.

"Where's Lalan?" asked Kunal casually.

"Out on a delivery too," snapped Sethji. "Get going ... or do you need a kick-start?"

Kunal grabbed the bag of food and walked out the door. One of these days he prayed he'd have the chance to kick-start Sethji to oblivion.

Chapter Four

Kunal glanced up and down the busy street as people brushed past in both directions. No one paid him the slightest attention.

He read the note — 12 Pandit Road. Not too far from Mangal Lane, the street the waiters were always talking about. He set off at a fast clip and reached a side street. Should he take the shortcut through the alley today? It would shave a few minutes off the delivery time. He hesitated. What if the hulk kept his word and was lying in wait for him? Kunal shook his head; he was just being silly.

Long fingers of shadow poked into the narrow alley. A stray dog nosed through a pile of putrid garbage. Darkness pooled in doorways of houses that were scrunched up against each other from one end of the alley to the other. Kunal took a deep breath and started walking.

He had reached halfway when something skittered past his legs. He stumbled. A black rat as large as a kitten disappeared into the shadows. He shuddered and walked faster, trying not to jerk the packet of food too much.

That's when he heard two sounds simultaneously: heavy

CORK CITY LIBRARIES

footsteps approaching from behind and the rattle of metal wheels on asphalt. He froze, remembering the beggar who haunted the *dhaba* and his nightmares. He was one of Abdulla's boys assigned this territory for begging. His legs had been cut off when he had been very young to make him more pitiable. He navigated the streets of Bombay on a wooden platform fitted with wheels, and delighted in waggling the disfigured stumps under the nose of anyone who wouldn't part with a rupee.

Kunal looked back. Cars and scooters, parked two deep in the narrow alley, obstructed his view of the entrance. He crouched behind the nearest car and peered out, pulse racing, mouth dry. The hot and humid air sat heavily on his shoulders. The whir of approaching wheels ricocheted off the walls, punctuated by a steady crunch of footsteps. Were they in this street or the next? The lanes were so close in this part of the city it was impossible to tell.

Suddenly, Kunal didn't want to find out. He jumped to his feet and sprinted the remainder of the way, bursting onto the main road on the other side, almost knocking a passerby off her feet.

"Ooof!" the woman yelped. "Watch where you're going!"

"Sorry," said Kunal. He clutched the packet of food to his chest, gasping for breath.

"What's the matter?" said the woman in a soft, calming voice. "You look as if you've seen a ghost."

People streamed past, bumping into them, cursing occasionally. Kunal did not answer. Instead, he peered into the deep gloom of the lane he'd just exited. No one came

30

out of the shadows. The woman followed his gaze.

"Is someone chasing you, boy? Do you want me to call the police?"

Kunal gulped in the warm night air, feeling foolish. At this rate he'd be jumping at shadows and sounds for the rest of his life. He had to learn to control his fears before they started to control him. He managed a weak smile. "It's nothing. I'm sorry!"

The woman watched him for a moment longer and then walked away shaking her head. Kunal waited at the curb, staring at the wet road that slowly pulsed amber, red, and green with the changing traffic lights. He crossed as soon as it was safe, and ran all the way to Pandit Road.

The customer had been slightly annoyed at the delay, but Kunal had made up a fatal accident, peppered it liberally with gruesome descriptions, and narrated it to the wide-eyed man who accepted the delivery. He had even managed to wangle a small tip and a lot of sympathy. Not bad for delivering cold food ... late!

His footsteps slowed as soon as he reached Mangal Lane. This place, halfway down the lane, was all the older boys talked about lately — a gaudy pink house that contained beautiful treasures within its damp walls. He knew they were talking about girls, though he'd never been inside. Only once had Sethji allowed him to accompany another waiter to deliver food to Mangal Lane and that was only because the order had been too large for one person to carry. The boy had made him wait at the doorstep while he went inside.

Should he go back to the *dhaba*, or stop and take a peek? At least then he would know exactly what made the boys so animated, maybe even join in the conversation.

He knew he was very late. The thought jabbed him like a warning finger in the chest. He had to get back to the *dhaba* or Sethji would beat him to pulp, but an invisible line was reeling him in. What *was* it that made the other boys' eyes sparkle? Why were they always fighting among themselves for deliveries to Mangal Lane? He had to find out.

Kunal threaded his way through the crowds, keeping a sharp lookout for anyone who might recognize him and snitch to Sethji. Just as he walked past a bar selling bootleg liquor, a familiar mop of hair caught his eye. He stopped. Through the haze of smoke he could make out a profile — Vinayak! At a bar in Mangal Lane? The old man was arguing with the bartender, demanding another drink. The slurred voice was so different from the one he heard in the mornings that for a moment Kunal could only stand and gape. Someone pushed past him and staggered into the bar. Kunal did not wait to see any more. It was really none of his business.

He paused at the foot of the steps of the Happy House, which was what the waiters called it. No one really looked very happy so he wondered how it got this name. People jostled past, their eyes fixed on the myriad women loitering in doorways and along the many balconies of the houses lining the street. Kids playing on the sidewalk called out to each other in shrill voices. Fragrances of food, cheap perfumes, and cigarette smoke lingered in the air.

Someone whistled at him. Kunal looked up and his heart skipped a beat. He had never laid eyes on a girl so pretty. Her black hair cascaded over her shoulders and her *kohl*-lined eyes lit up with a smile that made him feel warm inside. The *pallu* of her bright red *saree* spilled over the railing.

Kunal gaped at her, his heart pounding.

"You, boy! What are you doing?" a gruff voice called out.

Kunal started. At the door was a man, short but powerfully built. The muscles of his arms bulged through the sleeves of his T-shirt. His callused hands were as large as the plates at the *dhaba*. There was no doubt; one sock from this brute would be enough to knock him out.

The thug sauntered up to Kunal. "What are you doing loitering here? Go away!"

Kunal shook his head and gulped. "Who was that girl up there?" His eyes strayed upward again but the girl had vanished. His heart plummeted to his toes.

The thug grinned. "Chandni. She has that effect on anyone who lays eyes on her. Now get lost before I hand you your teeth. This is no place for children or beggars."

Kunal turned and fled, making up his mind to return as soon as he could.

Cursing himself for being stupid enough to be caught, Kunal headed back to the *dhaba* at a smart clip, aware that he was beyond late. By Sethji's standards he was I'd-strangle-you-if-I-could kind of late. His mind ran over all the excuses he'd made up in the past. Which one would work today? Overhead, thunder rumbled and white-hot lightning ripped through the sky. Another storm.

33

Keeping to the shadows, he crept up to the *dhaba*, but one of the waiters — Sethji's favourite — spied him. The miserable sycophant tapped Sethji on the shoulder and pointed towards Kunal before retreating to the kitchen. By the time Kunal reached the entrance, Sethji was at the door, chewing on a mouthful of abuses he was dying to spit out. He grabbed a handful of Kunal's shirt and slapped him so hard his teeth rattled.

"What the hell took you so long?" said Sethji. "Did you have to feed the customer yourself?"

"Sorry," said Kunal, putting on his well-practised hangdog look. "There was an accident near Pandit Road and the roads were closed so I had to find another way home and then I got lost —"

"Shut up!" snarled Sethji, smacking him once more before Kunal backed away, out of reach of his employer's lethal hands. "Where's my money?"

Kunal pulled the notes from his pocket and dropped them onto Sethji's palm. Sethji counted his change while Kunal stood silently on the sidewalk awaiting further instructions.

Something bumped against Kunal's leg. He glanced down and almost yelled out loud. Abdulla's crippled beggar was sitting on a wooden platform fitted with wheels, gazing up at him with his good eye. The other one was just a hollow socket as if someone had scooped the eye out and thrown it away. A tin cup nestled between the stumps of his legs. How had he missed the rattle of wheels? Kunal's legs went wobbly and he reached out for the wall to steady himself.

"Spare a rupee. God will bless you," said the boy in a

nasal sing-song voice as he rattled the tin. He reached out to touch Kunal, who jumped out of the way, ashamed and horrified all at once.

"Get off with you!" yelled Sethji. "There's not a paisa to waste. You think this *dhaba* runs on fresh air?"

The boy held his ground. "Then will you give me money for information?"

Kunal forced himself to meet the boy's eye. There was no sadness, just a depth that Kunal never thought he'd see in a child younger than him. Not only had the beggar-boy accepted this life, he seemed to be enjoying the reaction he caused because of his disfigurement.

"What kind of information?" said Sethji. "First tell me what it is and then I'll decide if it's worth anything."

"Uh-uh," said the beggar. "If I tell you, you won't pay me!" He rolled back and forth on the sidewalk. The sound grated on Kunal's nerves and he wanted to scream or throw something at that sly face.

"If you don't tell me, I'll break the remaining bones in your body," said Sethji. He took a step towards the boy, breathing heavily.

"It's about one of your waiters, the big, tall guy," said the boy, rolling backward hurriedly.

"What about him?" said Sethji, frowning. "He's out on a delivery."

Kunal's heart scrabbled frantically in his chest. "Lalan! You're talking about Lalan. Where is he?"

The boy rattled his tin cup and Kunal couldn't help but admire his guts. Even crippled and at a disadvantage, he did not miss an opportunity to milk the situation. Kunal groped in his pockets for a coin, found one, and threw it into the boy's tin. "Quick," he said. "Tell me. Has something happened to him?"

"In the next alley. Some boys jumped him, most probably for his money," said the beggar.

"Is he all right?" asked Kunal.

The boy shrugged. "You think I was going to wait around to find out?"

"I have to go to him," said Kunal. "Please, Sethji."

"Let him be, he'll come on his own," Sethji replied.

"Please," said Kunal. "He could be badly hurt. I have to go!"

"Stupid hulk," muttered Sethji. "Guzzling so much of my food, and still unable to take care of himself. Now I have to lose two boys at the busiest time of the evening. You'll put in an extra hour in the kitchen for this. Go, find that idiot!" He waved his hand and turned away.

Just then Lalan stepped into the light. "No need," he said softly.

Kunal stared at him. Bright-red blood dripped steadily from Lalan's nose, streaking his filthy, torn shirt. A bruised eye was slowly turning purple in his pale face. Lalan staggered in and collapsed into Kunal's outstretched arms. Kunal grunted but managed to remain on his feet.

"Did they get all my money?" said Sethji. He glared at Lalan, making no move to help.

Lalan nodded, wincing with pain. Kunal tightened his grip on his friend's large frame.

Sethji snorted. "This is coming out of your salary. Kunal, get him out of here before my customers see him and lose their appetites. Between the two of you, I'll go bankrupt."

Kunal started to drag Lalan towards the back of the *dhaba*.

"You see how lucky you are that we took you in, you wretch?" said Sethji. He smacked Kunal's head as he shuffled past. "Give me any trouble and I'll sell you to the Beggar King, Abdulla. Only then you'll realize how comfortable a life you've been leading."

Chapter Five

Another wet day was breathing its last. The rain had driven everyone indoors, if only for a cup of tea, and by eight o'clock in the evening the *dhaba* was at its peak of chaos.

Kunal glanced at the packed dining room through thick clouds of *beedi* smoke. Oil shone from the surfaces of the tables. The damp walls sucked up the light, making the room appear dimmer, and the floor was a palette of food stains. There was a large, reddish-brown patch near one of the tables — probably spilled *sambar*, but it looked like blood and reminded him of Lalan; the stained shirt, the swollen eye and broken nose. Kunal shuddered. It could easily have been him.

Someone slapped him on the shoulder.

"Stop daydreaming," said Mrs. Seth. "There are so many orders waiting to be served." She barked out directions to the waiters with military precision. No one had a moment's rest.

At the pickup counter, Kunal searched for the table number under a plate of steaming chicken biryani. A hot ladle seared his knuckles and he cried out loud. And there was Badri, his face framed by the grimy window. "Did that hurt?" he said. "So sorry! My hand slipped. But if you do exactly as I tell you, I'll be more careful."

Kunal stepped back, rubbing his hand. Things were definitely getting worse and he didn't know how to stop it. "Which table ordered the biryani?" he asked, trying to keep his voice steady. "I can't find the number." Seeing Badri reminded him of the nightmare he'd been having. About the tiffins full of eyes, Badri's eyes that were always trained on him.

Just then the kitchen helper appeared in the window, "Why are you standing there admiring the biryani? It's for table two. Go!"

Kunal delivered the biryani, barely aware of what he was doing. His mind thrashed wildly, an animal caught in a trap. How was he going to protect himself? He couldn't ask Mrs. Seth for help or advice. No; even if he convinced her that there was more to Badri than met the eye she didn't have the courage to stand up to her husband.

Vinayak? He only came to the *dhaba* for a brief time in the mornings. He wouldn't be of much help now.

Lalan! Of course, he should have thought of him right away. After he'd served one more customer, Kunal loitered in the corridor, which reeked of raw onions and stale spices. A few minutes later, Lalan walked in with a mountain of dirty plates and a colourful face — a black eye that was almost swollen shut and jaundice-yellow bruises adorning his jaws and cheeks.

"That looks really bad," said Kunal. "Couldn't you have taken a couple of days off?"

39

"I can't afford to," said Lalan. He spoke softly, barely opening his mouth. "You know how many family members I have to feed? I need my wages. Every last paisa of it."

Kunal nodded, wishing he was one of them. He would willingly have gone hungry just to belong to a family. He would have happily given up his own wages too, if he'd ever been paid.

"I have something important to tell you, Lalan."

"Now? Can't it wait? Mrs. Seth's in a bad mood."

Kunal shook his head.

"Okay, let's talk quickly," said Lalan. "I have something to tell you too." He glanced at Kunal then looked away. Kunal's stomach dropped. This seemed serious.

Lalan ducked into a deserted room beside the swinging kitchen doors that was used for washing up soiled pots and pans and dumped the dishes into the sink. Kunal followed, wrinkling his nose. The stink in there was nauseating.

"You go first," said Kunal, searching his friend's face for a clue.

"I'm leaving," said Lalan.

Kunal exhaled audibly, the tightness in his chest loosening. "Is that it? Of course you should," said Kunal. "You look terrible. But before you go can you please warn Badri to stop staring at me? He's acting very funny lately and I don't like it." Kunal stopped, realizing how stupid this must sound, yet he couldn't shake the feeling that Badri was bad news. And out of all the waiters who worked in the *dhaba*, he was the unlucky one that Badri had decided to bother.

Lalan was quiet for a moment. Outside, the noise

40

continued unabated. The swinging door squeaked incessantly as waiters hurried to and from the kitchen, the helper's voice rose and fell as he called out the orders that were ready for pickup, and Mrs. Seth's military staccato filled in the gaps.

Lalan shook his head slightly and winced.

"Sorry," said Kunal. "I shouldn't be asking this of you today. Not when you're in so much pain. Go home; I'll handle Badri till you return. But when you do, you've got to help get him off my back. Okay?"

Lalan still did not smile. The bubble of fear in Kunal's chest expanded.

"You don't understand, Kunal. I'm leaving for good."

Kunal stared into Lalan's good eye. "You're joking," he said. "Please tell me you're joking."

Lalan put his hands on Kunal's shoulder and squeezed. "Sorry, my friend. But my father has found a better paying job for me. I can't stay here, especially after this." Lalan touched his face lightly. "Sethji barely feeds us crumbs and makes it look like he's doing us a big favour. And he refuses to pay up for his waiters' protection to the local gang. That's why they attack us at random and steal his money. Be extra careful while making deliveries. Okay?"

"You can't leave, Lalan," said Kunal. "You can't leave me here alone." He started to blubber and turned away, clutching the edge of the filthy sink. A large brown cockroach scooted out of the way.

He felt Lalan's breath on the back of his neck. "I have to, Kunal. I've made up my mind."

"I won't survive," whispered Kunal. He wiped his dripping

41

nose on his sleeve. "The rest of the waiters hate me. I've never been one of them. They'll gang up on me and make my life miserable. You know what I mean —"

Lalan turned him around. "You will survive. You have to. Now stop being an idiot and start acting your age."

"Get lost," snapped Kunal. "You're deserting me! You have no right to tell me anything now."

Lalan sighed. "Don't be mad at me, Kunal. I wish I could take you with me. But I can't. You'll have to learn to trust only yourself. It's the only way to survive in this city."

Kunal hated him for that second. Hated the way his best friend was gazing at him with such pity. As if he really cared. "Who else knows you're leaving?" he asked. "Have you told anyone yet?"

"A couple of boys in the kitchen know, so Badri probably knows, too," said Lalan. "Why?"

That explained why Badri had become bolder. Kunal felt like a moth caught in a fist that was rapidly closing. "So I'm the last person to know, and you call yourself a friend?" said Kunal. He couldn't keep the bitterness from his voice.

"I-I wanted to tell you ... properly," said Lalan. "I'm sorry."

"I have to go," Kunal mumbled, and fled.

"Wait ...," Lalan called out. Kunal ignored him.

He escaped through the back door into the alley and stood under the awning gulping in lungfuls of air, heavily laden with the smell of rotting garbage. Inhale, exhale, inhale, exhale. The rain was heavier than ever and within minutes his face was bathed in a cool mist.

Lalan was leaving. The betrayal twisted his gut. His friend was abandoning him. His own family wouldn't ever do this. He thought of his mother's glass bangle tucked safely under his mattress and wished he had it with him right now, just for something to hold on to.

"Hey, idiot! Stop admiring the garbage. Sethji's looking for you," the kitchen helper called out from the doorway. "Delivery."

Kunal wiped his face hastily and walked straight through to the front. Sethji glared at him as soon as he reached the counter. "Taking a break during your work time, *henh*? You'll work an extra hour tonight; help Badri clean up the kitchen."

The fist clenched tighter, crushing him. He could barely breathe.

"Where am I taking this?" said Kunal.

Sethji held out a piece of paper with an address. Kunal snatched it from his hand without looking at it. He was desperate to flee the *dhaba*, escape these four walls that had meant nothing but pain and humiliation to him. He picked up the food and walked out into the pouring rain.

When he was out of sight of the *dhaba*, Kunal paused and looked at the piece of paper in his hand. It was rapidly becoming soggy, but he didn't care.

"*I'm leaving for good.*" Lalan's voice echoed in his head.

He shivered. He was on his own now. With the waiters. And Sethji. And Badri.

The rain fell in thick, warm sheets. Kunal looked at the paper again; a wet wad on his palm. He spread his fingers and let the paper wash away. As the flecks of white hurtled through a rivulet of water running along the sidewalk and disappeared into the sewers of Bombay, he was filled with a sense of foreboding.

He couldn't stay on at the *dhaba*. He had to leave. He knew this with a certainty he had not felt in a long time. He couldn't roam the streets, either. If Lalan, large as he was, could get brutally beaten up, what chance did he have? He looked around. People rushed past, intent on getting out of the pouring rain. Kunal felt eyes on him. Were they real or in his mind? He had to keep moving. One sign of weakness and they'd take him down.

There was only one other option. Ever since Vinayak had given his address, Kunal had kept it in his pocket, wrapped in a bit of plastic for a rainy day. And that day had arrived. But even as he made his decision, the image of Vinayak in the bar popped into his head. He pushed it away; he had nowhere else to go. It was that or life on the streets.

Kunal headed to the nearest alley. A mangy dog, with fur plastered to its thin body, rooted around in the corners for scraps. He whistled. It looked up. Kunal knelt and undid the package of food. The dog sniffed the air and sidled up cautiously. It came closer, licking its lips. Then it let out a small whine and wagged its tail.

"Come on," urged Kunal. "I won't hurt you."

The dog stayed out of reach, eyeing the food and then Kunal. Drool glistened at the corners of its mouth but it did not come any closer. *I know how you feel*, thought Kunal. *Better to be cautious than stupid. Trust no one.* He stood up and stepped away from the food. The dog shuffled closer, still eyeing him warily.

"Enjoy," said Kunal, and he walked away. When he glanced back, the dog was scarfing twenty rupees worth of Sethji's food with gusto.

Kunal smiled.

Chapter Six

Kunal stood shivering in the narrow corridor on the third floor of the *chawl* and looked around him. The courtyard he had just crossed was pockmarked with hollows of darkness. A solitary streetlight at the entrance illuminated slashes of silver rain. Barely anyone was about on the streets; but, more important, no one had followed him. He turned back to face the door with the large black five on it.

Did he dare knock? Would Vinayak be happy or annoyed to see him? Kunal put his ear to the door and heard the clink of a glass but no voices. He took a deep breath and knocked. Someone stood up. There was a crash. Then footsteps. The door flew open, bathing him in yellow light. The stink of cheap alcohol greeted him before Vinayak did.

"Vinayakji?" said Kunal. He moved closer.

The old man peered at him, swaying slightly. "Kunal? What are you doing here?"

"I want to stay the night with you," said Kunal. "Please, may I come in?" A sneeze shook him from head to toe.

"Come in, come in," said Vinayak. "How silly of me to keep you standing outside in this miserable weather." His tongue slipped over the words as if they were coated with grease. *So different from his crisp speech in the mornings,* Kunal thought.

Vinayak's room was stark. A single naked bulb hung from the centre of the room. White-washed walls encircled them, except for a large damp spot under the window where water had seeped in. A rickety table with two chairs stood in a corner of the room facing an L-shaped counter that might have been a kitchenette at one time but was now bare. One chair was overturned and Kunal immediately righted it.

There was a door at the back of the room and a wooden cupboard beside it. Near the leg of the only cot in the room was a bottle of amber liquid and a half-filled glass.

Vinayak unhooked a towel from behind the door and threw it at him. "Dry yourself. I'll get you some clothes." He walked unsteadily to the cupboard and pulled out a white *kurta* and pyjamas. "The bathroom's right through this door."

"Thank you," said Kunal. He hurried into the bathroom, towelling his hair. His wet shorts and shirt clung to him, raising goosebumps.

Moments later, dry and warm in oversized clothes, he squatted on the floor in front of Vinayak.

"Kunal, my friend, life is tough," said Vinayak. He rotated his glass, staring at the liquid that swirled perilously close to the rim. "You need three things to survive in this crazy city of ours — family, friends, and money."

Kunal's stomach clenched. He had none of the things Vinayak had just mentioned. No family, no friends, and not a single rupee.

"But why are you drinking?" said Kunal. "I thought you had everything." This was a side of Vinayak he had never seen before and wished he didn't have to. He preferred the morning version of the old man.

"Ahhhh, it's a long story," said Vinayak. He looked out the window. Kunal followed his gaze, and watched the rain splash on the windowsill. "Some day I'll share it. But for now, tell me, why are you here?"

"I've run away and I'm not going back," said Kunal. "Please don't make me."

Vinayak slurped the amber liquid. "Kunal, no one can make you do anything you don't want to. Remember that. Life is too short —"

Kunal cut in, sensing a rambling speech coming up. "May I stay here for a few days? Could you help me find a job? As a *dabbawalla*?

Vinayak drained the remaining liquid in one swallow and shuddered as if he'd just downed bitter medicine. He leaned forward and shoved the glass under the cot, almost toppling with the effort. "We could try. But I must warn you, the *dabbawallas* only recruit from their own community." His bleary eyes tried to focus on Kunal as he spoke.

"They won't give anyone else a chance?" asked Kunal. "Even if the person is willing to work hard?"

"I really don't know," said Vinayak with a huge yawn. "We'll see. But don't worry your head about it now. You have me, and I'm sure you've got a little saved up from all those tips at the *dhaba*, right? I'll find you a job even if it takes some time.

"But you're so high up in the organization," said Kunal. "Surely they'll listen to you."

Vinayak eyes were suddenly moist. He reached out a trembling hand and stroked Kunal's cheek. It was so unexpected that Kunal drew back, regretting it almost instantly. This was the first time anyone had touched him this way — gently. He swallowed the lump that constricted his throat.

"I'll help you in any way I can, my ..." Vinayak didn't finish the sentence. His eyelids started to droop. He lay down on his cot. "Very tired. Talk ... morning."

"Thank you, Vinayakji," said Kunal. "You won't regret it. I promise. I'll work hard." He stopped.

Vinayak was already snoring. Kunal realized he had known this man for four years and yet he really did not know him at all. He had no idea what Vinayak was like when he was not working. But it had been this tired old man who, on learning that Kunal had never attended school, had taught him to read and write by smuggling an alphabet book and writing paper to him, and always looking out for him. He did not know why but he knew this old man was fond of him. His anxiety subsided a little. Vinayak couldn't be all that bad, even if he was fond of drinking every night.

Kunal wandered over to the window, too wound up to sleep.

How could he have been so stupid? He had left the *dhaba* without any money or his mother's bangle, still hidden under his mattress. Would Mrs. Seth throw it out when she found it? The thought was unbearable!

Around him, the lights in the *chawl* were going out, one by one. A spray of rain bathed his hot face. He knew what he had to do. He had to go back not only to get some money, but also the only keepsake his mother had left for him. And he had to do it tonight.

He glanced at the snoring figure. He could go to the *dhaba*, grab what he needed, and be back within an hour. Vinayak would never know. Kunal changed back into his wet clothes, hating their cold and damp embrace. He tiptoed to the door and pulled it open. The rain had slowed to a drizzle. The street appeared soft and blurry, almost beautiful, in the diffused lamplight. He stepped out, feeling as if he were walking into a dream sequence of a Bollywood movie, shut the door, and ran all the way back to Sethji's.

By the time Kunal reached the *dhaba*, the rain had stopped. It was an hour before midnight and the *dhaba* was emptying slowly.

From the shadow of a building across the street, Kunal watched Sethji ingratiate himself with the customers as he counted the money and handed back their change. He was extremely witty and funny at this moment and Kunal and all the waiters knew it was because he was short-changing the customers and hoping to distract them. If Sethji could get away with even ten paise per customer, he'd be several rupees richer by the end of the day. Of course, not all the customers were daft. Some counted their change before leaving and demanded their correct due.

Kunal squatted on the doorstep trying to ignore the aroma of biryani, curry, and fresh naan that wafted towards him from across the street. He regretted donating the food to that stray now, but what was done was done. Instead, he focused on his plan to get the money owed to him. He had worked in the *dhaba* since he could stand on his feet — at first in the kitchen peeling potatoes or cleaning up, and then as a waiter. He leaned back against the door, remembering countless evenings on his hands and knees, scrubbing the filthy floors, the stink of soap and phenyl sharp in his nose. He had laboured for the Seths for years, but they had never paid him. Sometimes they let him keep the tips, but those occasions were few and far between.

He was going to raid the cash register and take what was due to him. Just to be fair, he deducted a bit for food and lodging. Even with that, the Seths owed him thousands of rupees. He doubted the cash register would hold that much, but on a good day it would have at least two thousand. He had once observed Sethji putting another little bundle of notes in the drawer below the cash register. He meant to take that too.

That should be more than enough to tide him over till Vinayak found him a job.

A foul-smelling beggar lurched past, probably looking for a place to sleep. Kunal wrinkled his nose and shrank further into the shadow, wishing closing time would come soon. He would have just a few minutes when Sethji went to the kitchen to discuss the next day's menu with Badri and keep an eye on the evening shift of waiters so that they didn't eat too much of the leftovers, which could be served to customers the next day. At this time the cash register was unattended and the *dhaba* would be empty.

Just the thought of it made his throat dry. He had never stolen anything in his life — not even food on the days the Seths had punished him for some minor infraction. But he told himself that if he took what was owed to him, it wasn't stealing. The other waiters got paid. All he was doing was paying himself.

Almost midnight. The last customer walked out of the *dhaba* without checking his change. Sethji called out an extra cheery goodbye. He'd probably got away with twenty paisa of this man's change. Kunal wiped his sweaty hands on his almost dry clothes and crossed the road at a sprint.

He hid behind a large mound of garbage on the sidewalk, his heart pounding. *He'll do the same thing he does each night and you'll have at least five minutes to get the money and run. Nothing simpler.*

Sethji took his time counting the money and making notes in his little notebook, which he carried at all times. Kunal inhaled the pungent fumes of the rotting garbage and his eyes watered. Sweat glued his shirt to his back as he waited for Sethji to leave.

Sethji waddled out from behind the counter. Kunal tensed, ready to sprint. But Sethji didn't walk into the kitchen. He came towards the door and peered out into the darkness. Kunal almost stopped breathing. Did Sethji sense he was there? If he took a few more steps, he'd see Kunal crouched behind the garbage. Sweat poured into his eyes, blinding him, and he was starting to feel nauseous. *Go, please go*, Kunal prayed.

On cue, Sethji turned and walked into the kitchen. Kunal jumped to his feet and almost lost his balance. He was light-headed with panic as he hurried towards the till, keeping low to the ground. The door to the kitchen swung gently in Sethji's wake and then it was still. Kunal raced behind the counter and opened the cash register. Piles of fifties, tens, and fives, lay in their compartments. Kunal had never seen so much money in his life. *Grab them now*, he told himself, *you can count them later*. He scooped up all the cash and stuffed it into his pocket, one eye trained on the kitchen door.

Kunal opened the drawer below and found another roll of notes. Someone up there was on his side today. This was a good haul; he was sure he had at least three thousand rupees and Sethji would never suspect him. He felt a pang as he realized the other waiters would bear the brunt of Sethji's wrath when he discovered he had been robbed, but dismissed it almost immediately. Other than Lalan, no one had ever cared about him, so why should he care about them?

Kunal hurried out from behind the counter and was at the entrance when a thought arrested his steps. His mother's bangle. Did he dare get that, too? He knew he had been incredibly lucky so far. He should run and get out now. While he still had the chance. But he hesitated, unable to leave behind the only thing that belonged to his mother.

At that moment the door swung open and Sethji walked into the room with his sycophant, Raju, trailing behind him like a dog.

"YOU!" snarled Sethji. "Where have you been all this while? You're coming back from the delivery just now?"

Kunal's legs were frozen. His brains were frozen. He was sure the guilt of his recent act was all over his face. Sethji's eyes strayed to the open drawer of the cash register. Kunal realized he had forgotten to shut it! Sethji bellowed and came at him with surprising speed. He lashed out and Kunal went sprawling onto the floor.

"Raju, I want you to get all the waiters and leave," said Sethji in a very calm voice. "Use the back entrance. Go now!"

Raju nodded and turned away, but not before Kunal saw the huge grin plastered on his face. Once the kitchen door swung shut behind him, Sethji grabbed a handful of Kunal's shirt and pulled him to his feet. "Did you steal from me?"

"Please, Sethji, I was only taking the wages due to me," Kunal blubbered. "Nothing more. The other waiters get paid and I —"

Sethji slapped him so hard, he tasted blood. "Shut up and empty your pockets."

With shaking hands Kunal removed the bundles of notes and laid them on the counter. Sethji's black eyes were like stones as they observed him. *Why had he stopped? Why had he hesitated? He would have been halfway to Vinayak's by now.*

Sethji shoved Kunal so hard that down he went on the floor again, banging his head against a chair. Yet he could see Sethji clearly enough, and the expression on his employer's face chilled him to the core.

Chapter Seven

Sethji kicked Kunal in the face. Kunal screamed, sure it had shattered into a million pieces. Blood flooded his mouth, spilling onto his shirt and the floor. He stared at the bright red pool in horror, almost overcome with the urge to vomit and faint at the same time.

Sethji pulled the shutter down and locked it. An impenetrable wall of steel stood between him and freedom. Kunal watched Sethji, his heart banging against his rib cage. What would happen to him now?

Ignoring Kunal, Sethji stepped over to the counter, put the money back into the cash register and locked it, then bowed his head and prayed to the assorted figurines of deities displayed behind the counter. Kunal prayed too.

When Sethji had finished, he advanced on Kunal. The glint in his eye was unmistakable. Kunal slid backward till he reached a wall. He put up his hands to ward off the blows he knew were coming. "Please spare me," he said. "The gods won't forgive you if you hurt someone deliberately."

A slow smile spread across Sethji's face. "Don't you worry about me," he said. "I've already asked for forgiveness for what I'm about to do."

The walls closed in around Kunal.

The door squeaked, disturbing the stagnant air in the dark room.

Kunal dragged himself up from the depths of sleep, trying to shake off the heavy stupor that pulled at him. He attempted to sit up. Pain ripped through him. He lay still, sweating, afraid to move a muscle.

"Kunal," came an urgent whisper.

It was Mrs. Seth. *Did she want a turn at bashing him up, too?* Kunal tried to scrunch lower into the bed. Tears leaked out of the corners of his eyes and he hated himself for being so weak. And so stupid.

Mrs. Seth closed the door quietly behind her and switched on the light. She sat on his bed and stared at him. Kunal was relieved to see she did not look angry, only anxious.

"You have to leave tonight," she said.

Kunal's body ached just at the thought of sitting up, let alone running away. Every breath brought a fresh wave of fiery pain. "I don't understand. Sethji is letting me go?"

Mrs. Seth closed her eyes. When she opened them again they were soft, and filled with deep anguish. "He's selling you to Abdulla. He wants to make an example of you so that no waiter will ever be tempted to steal from him again. They'll finalize the deal tonight. Everyone wins," she whispered, "except you."

"No!" said Kunal. He struggled to sit up. The effort almost made him pass out. "No," he repeated weakly. "Please don't let him sell me, Mrs. Seth ... I'm sorry ... so very sorry ..."

"I won't let him," said Mrs. Seth. She clasped his hands in hers. "Don't you worry."

It was her tone more than her words that were his undoing. She had never spoken to him with such tenderness. Huge, ragged sobs burst out of him. He could barely breathe.

Mrs. Seth hugged him tight. He cried harder.

"I wish Sethji had killed me," Kunal gasped. "I don't want to be a beggar. I don't want to be mutilated by Abdulla. I wish I was dead."

Mrs. Seth hugged him tighter. "You stupid boy," she said, her voice cracking. "This is not your fault. If only I hadn't agreed to help your mother, your life might have been so very different."

Kunal froze. With a huge effort he clamped down on the sobs, pulled away, and stared at her. She was staring at him, too, her face deathly pale. He opened his mouth but no words came out. Mrs. Seth stood up but Kunal reached out and pulled her down again.

"You knew my mother?"

Her face turned whiter. "No."

"You're lying! You just said you did."

"I have to make arrangements to get you out of here. We have very little time."

"Please, Mrs. Seth. Just tell me the truth." His face crumpled and he dropped his head in her lap. "I'm not an orphan after all? I have family?"

She gripped his shoulder and pushed him away. "Be strong, Kunal. This world is not kind to the weak-hearted."

Kunal raised his head. "Easy for you to say. You have everything, and yet you won't allow me a little bit of happiness? Tell me where she is."

Mrs. Seth did not answer. She stood up quickly and went to the door. This time Kunal did not stop her. Anger had replaced the horror from a few moments ago.

"Liar," he said softly. "You lied when you said I was an orphan. You've lied to me all my life."

Mrs. Seth whirled around, her face red. "So what if I did? I did it for your own good. I'm sick of this mess. And it all started with your mother when she lied to me. She's the liar, not me."

"How so?" asked Kunal.

"I have to go," repeated Mrs. Seth. She paused, looked back. "When you didn't return to the *dhaba* after the delivery last evening I was sure you had run away. You had, hadn't you?"

Kunal knew the answer was on his face.

"Why did you come back, Kunal? Why didn't you just stay away? You've made matters worse."

"I came for what was owed to me," said Kunal. "I needed the money to survive." He was trembling so much he had to hug himself to stop the shaking. "But if I hadn't, I would never have known that I have family, that I'm not an orphan. The beating was worth it! Please tell me where she is. I'll go away and never trouble you again."

Kunal swung his feet to the floor and almost toppled over.

"Stay there!" snapped Mrs. Seth. She made him lie down again. "You're in no condition to walk. But there are only two hours to closing. Sethji is meeting Abdulla after the customers have gone. He'll hand you over with all the waiters watching. No one, not even I, can stop him then." She bit her trembling lip. "After that, there's no hope ... none at all." The last words were so soft, it was almost as if she were speaking to herself.

"I'll go to Vinayak's," said Kunal. "That's where I ran away to, earlier."

Mrs. Seth hurried to the door. "You'd better go back there immediately. I'll call Vinayak to come get you. Talk to no one about this."

"And my mother?"

"Forget about her. She's forgotten about you."

"But why?" asked Kunal, his heart and head aching ferociously. "Why did she just leave me with you?"

Mrs. Seth was quiet for a moment and Kunal held his breath, praying she would go on.

"We were the best of friends once," she said softly. "In school. No secrets and no lies between us. Then we grew up and lost touch till the time I found you on my doorstep. She did not even have the courage to face me."

Kunal's lungs were burning for air. He took in a deep shuddering breath, his ribs aching with the effort. "And you never saw her after that?"

"No," said Mrs. Seth, a hardness in her voice.

"But why?"

"If you don't want to be found, you live in a big city like Bombay."

The words hurt more than the bruises all over Kunal's

body. "You're wrong," he shouted. "You hear me? Wrong!"

"Maybe I am," said Mrs. Seth. She reached out and touched his face gently. "All I can say right now is that your future lies with Vinayak. I will do everything I can to get you out safely. Don't expect anything else from me."

And before Kunal could say another word she was gone. The room spun gently around him. Kunal closed his eyes and his hand sought out the green bangle tucked under the edge of his mattress. His fingertips moved over its smooth surface, one thought pulsing within him: he had family. He belonged to someone.

"Kunal, wake up."

Someone was shaking him. He opened his eyes — the room was dark.

Terror flooded him. Was Abdulla here already?

"Who ... who is it?" he said.

"It's me, Kunal. You don't have to worry."

He recognized the voice now. "Vinayakji?"

The room was coming into focus, illuminated by the dim glow from the streetlights.

"Yes. Where did you go to last night?" said Vinayak. He sat down on the bed and ran a shaky hand through his hair. "I was worried when I woke up this morning and found you gone. It's Saturday, so I had no reason to come here. If I had, it would have made Sethji suspicious. All day I've thought about you, wondering what to do when I heard from Mrs. Seth." The words tumbled out of him in short, jerky phrases. "Is this how you treat a friend?"

60

"I'm sorry," whispered Kunal, "but when you mentioned that a person needed money to survive, I realized I didn't have any. I didn't want to be a burden on you, so —"

Vinayak shook his head. "So you put yourself in danger again? Do you think so little of me?"

Kunal swallowed the lump in his throat. He couldn't trust himself to speak.

"We have to get you out of here immediately. Mrs. Seth told me about Abdulla."

Kunal sat up immediately. The world tilted, then righted itself. "I just need to go to the bathroom and then we can leave."

"Hurry," said Vinayak. "I'll pack your things."

Kunal gritted his teeth as he walked to the bathroom. It was like walking on a live wire. He splashed his face with cool water, gargled, and spat out the ugly taste of blood that coated his tongue. Mrs. Seth knew who his mother was, probably knew where she lived. If he left now, he would never find out. But if he didn't leave now, Abdulla would maim him for life. The boy without legs slid into his mind. By tomorrow he might be traversing some road in Bombay on a wheeled platform too. Kunal retched into the basin.

When he returned, Vinayak was pacing the room, bundle in hand. "Ready? Let's go."

Kunal glanced out the window. Streetlights kept the deep darkness at bay. His eyes searched for the red rag on the TV antenna. Found it. The rag fluttered once, then fell limp. He'd go with Vinayak, but he would find a way to come back and ask Mrs. Seth for his mother's address.

The door to his room opened. Kunal involuntarily moved closer to Vinayak, the bruises on his body flaring with pain.

Mrs. Seth walked into the room. Kunal's heart leaped. Maybe she'd changed her mind.

"Here's what you came for, Kunal," said Mrs. Seth. "I couldn't take too much or Sethji would have noticed, but it'll help till you get on your own feet." She thrust a wad of notes into his hands. "May Lord Ganesh remove every obstacle from your path. And, Vinayak, you're a good man. Thank you."

Vinayak nodded.

Kunal stared at the notes uncomprehendingly. He knew she was taking a huge risk for him and he should thank her but at the moment his only thought was about his mother, and finding out her name.

"I'm taking this bangle too," said Kunal. He held up the green bangle and then tucked it quickly into his pocket. "I hope you don't mind. It's the only thing I have left that belonged to my mother." He hoped he had injected enough bitterness and sadness in his voice to shame her into telling him what he wanted to know.

Mrs. Seth stared at him for a moment. "It's not your mother's — it's mine. But you can have it."

Kunal's heart shrivelled inside his chest. It was Mrs. Seth who had told him the bangle was once his mother's. Another lie. The one thing that had comforted him during his darkest moments hadn't been real. The one thing that had stopped him from fleeing the *dhaba*, and earned him the worst beating of his life, had not been worth the trouble.

"We're wasting time," said Vinayak. "Whatever it is you need to know can wait. Right now we have to move."

Kunal grasped Mrs. Seth's arm. "You have to tell me —"

Mrs. Seth shook his hand off. "Stop it, Kunal! Sethji is in a murderous mood. All the waiters and the kitchen staff have heard about the incident and they're laughing at him. There are only a couple of customers left in the *dhaba* and Abdulla could very well get here early. Follow me."

Vinayak pushed Kunal towards the door. They tiptoed across the corridor and Kunal shot a glance at the dining room below. The whirring fan and the edges of the grimy tables came into view. One of the waiters was mopping the floor and the antiseptic smell of phenyl wafted up to him. Muted voices came from the kitchen. Then they were past and into the Seths' bedroom. Mrs. Seth unlocked a black door on the far side of the room.

"This leads straight to the alley. Be quick. Good luck, and don't come back," she said, almost pushing Kunal out. They stepped through the door and the bolt shot back into place. They descended the dark staircase.

"What was all that about?" said Vinayak as they hurried towards the bright lights at the mouth of the alley.

"I'm sorry, Vinayakji. I don't feel like talking right now," said Kunal. "I'll explain later." Each step became harder to take because he knew he was deliberately walking away from the truth, from the one chance at having a real family.

He stopped abruptly. He had never been one to give up easily.

"I can't leave!" said Kunal. "I have to do this now,

Vinayakji. I may never get another chance." He ran back, ignoring the pain that shimmied up and down his spine.

"Come back, you idiot!" yelled Vinayak. "It's not safe!"

Kunal didn't even slow down. He raced up the steps to the black door and hammered on it with both fists.

The door flew open a few seconds later and there was Mrs. Seth, white-faced and trembling. "Are you mad?" Her hand shook and the piece of paper in her hand fluttered. "Did you not hear a word I said?"

"I must know about my mother," said Kunal. "I'm not leaving till you tell me. I *can't*."

"Why won't you just leave it alone, Kunal?" said Mrs. Seth in a choked whisper. "Haven't you suffered enough? The truth will only hurt you more."

"I don't care," he said. "I'd rather be miserable knowing the truth than live a lie for the rest of my life."

They both heard the thump of footsteps climbing the stairs. Mrs. Seth looked ready to faint. She clutched her heart, took a deep breath, and thrust the paper she was holding at him. "Here's the letter your mother wrote when she left you at my doorstep. I never heard from her again. Though I tried hard to track her down, it was futile. All I could find out was that she was still in Bombay."

Kunal took the letter from her and scanned it. It was signed *Anahita*. There was no last name, no address. He crammed it into his pocket. The footsteps had reached the top of the steps. It could be no other than Sethji.

"Her full name?" said Kunal. "Do you know where I can find her?"

"Anahita Patel. A couple of years ago someone told me she was working as a financial analyst downtown. There are thousands of A. Patels in the phonebook so I didn't bother to check if it was really her. Please go!"

Kunal lunged forward and hugged Mrs. Seth tight.

She hugged him back. The door flew open. Sethji's bulk filled the entrance. He bellowed with rage, stomping towards them. "Gurpreet, what the hell are you doing? And what is this thief doing in our room? I'll teach this boy a lesson he'll remember for the rest of his life."

"No!" said Mrs. Seth, shielding Kunal. "I won't let you."

"In that case, you need the first lesson, you wretched woman." Sethji's face was terrifying as he advanced on them, tugging at his moustache viciously.

Mrs. Seth turned around, pushed Kunal out the door and slammed it in his face. Her scream echoed through the thin wood. Then there was silence.

As Kunal walked alongside Vinayak in the darkness, he knew he would never forget Mrs. Seth's last words to him. Or her scream.

Chapter Eight

My dear Gurpreet,

I'm in trouble and I need your help. I'm leaving my son, Kunal, with you so that I can look for his father, Anurag. I used to pack his tiffin lunch. We got to know each other well and I fell in love. He loved me too, I know he did. But when I sent a note in his tiffin to tell him I was pregnant, I never heard back. I don't know what happened.

Of course, I was in such a panic when he didn't reply that I broke down. Mother suspected something was wrong and forced me to tell her what it was. Then she went completely mad. Took me to Panchgani, where I've been these last few months, and had the baby. Mother doesn't believe in abortions and thank God for it, because I know something happened which prevented my sweet Anurag from answering my letter. That day my regular dabbawalla *was ill and a substitute was delivering the* dabbas. *Maybe he lost the tiffin.*

So here I am, back in Bombay. Mother was intent on dropping Kunal off at an orphanage, first in Panchgani and now here in Bombay. I won't allow it. After all, he's my child! I'll track down Anurag and we'll be a family.

Please look after my darling Kunal. It's only for a week, but it'll give us a chance to be a family. I know I'm assuming a lot, Gurpreet, but I also know a good friend like you will not deny me this chance to find happiness.

One week is all I'm asking for and then he'll be off your hands. I'll be in your debt forever. Tell Kunal I love him.

You take care,

Anahita

Chapter Nine

The tinkling of a prayer bell woke Kunal. Shafts of sunlight beamed at him through the bars on the window. Sleep receded and the world around him came into focus; a clean white room swirling with golden light, honks of impatient traffic from outside, a hint of sandalwood incense perfuming the air, and hard tile digging into his back.

He sat up. He was still sore, but a good night's sleep had made the pain bearable. The events of the previous night flooded his head and the sunshine lost some of its golden sheen. He had hidden the letter Mrs. Seth had thrust at him, unable to show it to Vinayak last night. It was his mother's and he wanted to read it first. And he had, standing in the tiny bathroom in Vinayak's room. The short letter revealed so much: the mistake his mother had made as a teenager by getting pregnant out of wedlock; his father's name; how he had ended up with Mrs. Seth; but above all, the fact that his mother loved him.

But why hadn't she returned in a week? What happened? Did she find his father? Were they together now? The one week had turned into thirteen years and she still hadn't returned. There were so many questions and no answers.

His thoughts turned to Mrs. Seth. How must she have felt, saddled with a child she hadn't even asked for? He shook his head, trying to rid himself of the image of her as he'd fled the *dhaba*. Her piercing shriek still echoed in his ears. Was she all right?

He slipped the green bangle from his pocket and ran his fingers over its glassy surface. Mrs. Seth had given him something to hold on to, something to believe in even though she had lost all hope that his mother, her friend, would ever return. And for a moment he was glad she had lied. That green bangle had helped him through many a dark moment. And then there was the money she had given him last night. In her own way she had loved him and he would never get the chance to thank her. He blinked back tears that threatened to spill out.

But he had to look for his mother now. He had to find out the truth, no matter how painful. He couldn't live with a lie any longer. And no matter how many A. Patels there were in Bombay, he would find the right one, even if it took him forever.

Unable to sit still, he got to his feet. It was still early, only seven in the morning by Vinayak's old watch that lay on the floor beside his cot, but already the heat had bite. Cool tile pressed against the soles of his feet as he padded to the window and looked out at the *chawl*.

The U-shaped building embraced a bare patch of earth with a lone, scraggly tree at its centre. Impaled on its topmost branch were the tattered remains of a red kite. Women were lining up near the communal tap in the centre of the yard to stock up on water before the supply was cut off for the day. Plastic buckets lay scattered around them like colourful flowers. They gossiped and laughed as they awaited their turn.

Kunal peered out through the bars. On either side, doors lined the corridor as far as he could see. A balcony with steel railings ran the length of the narrow corridor overlooking the courtyard. In front of every room, an assortment of clothes hung from flimsy lines attached to the railing.

"You okay?" said Vinayak softly.

Kunal started and turned around.

Vinayak lay in bed, cradling his head in his hands, watching him.

"I think so," said Kunal. A comfortable silence stretched between them.

"Do you want to talk about last night?" asked Vinayak. He sat up and swung his feet to the floor. "You seemed very upset. Why did you run back?"

Kunal shook his head, annoyed at the sudden lump in his throat. He wasn't ready to talk about this yet, not even with Vinayak. He glanced out the window and asked the first question that popped into his head. "How many people live in this *chawl*?"

"It was made for about a hundred people but three hundred actually live here," said Vinayak.

"I see," said Kunal. He couldn't think of anything else to say.

A man dressed in a holey vest and shorts walked past

the window with a mug of water and a newspaper tucked under his arm. His eyes flicked towards Kunal briefly as he passed. Within minutes, another walked past. He too was carrying a mug of water and a newspaper.

Kunal looked at Vinayak. "Surely they're not going to the train station for ... to ... er ... you know what I mean."

Vinayak had a twinkle in his eye. "Only ten rooms in this *chawl* have an attached bathroom. The rest have to use the communal toilets located at either end of the corridors on each floor. Twenty years of service with the *dabbawallas* has earned me one, or by now we'd be lining up on the landing with a mug of water just like these people. Every week someone is beaten up or forcibly dragged out because he took too long."

"Are you serious?" said Kunal. He had to smile.

"Maybe, maybe not!" said Vinayak. He massaged his legs, sighing. Thick blue ropes of varicose veins snaked up his legs and into his pyjamas, bunched up at the knees. "Thank God it's Sunday," he said, stifling a yawn. "We'll get you settled before I go to work on Monday."

"Will you help me find a job?" asked Kunal. "I can't sit around doing nothing."

"One thing at a time. Let's get some breakfast first," said Vinayak. He scratched the mass of grey curls that peeped from the open neck of his rumpled *kurta*. "I'm hungry."

"I'm not," said Kunal. The thought of food reminded him of the *dhaba*. And Mrs. Seth. If he were still there, he'd be serving breakfast to the crowds with her hovering over them, barking out orders. Sundays were particularly busy at the *dhaba* and, in spite of everything, he longed to hear her voice once more.

"I'll ask you that question when a plate of the best breakfast in Bombay is in front of you," said Vinayak.

"You'll make breakfast here?" asked Kunal. His eyes flicked to the bare counter at the back of the room.

"No one uses this kitchen now," said Vinayak abruptly. "We'll be eating out."

Before Kunal could ask why, Vinayak had walked into the bathroom and shut the door. There was so much about Vinayak he did not know and wasn't sure if he should ask. Where was his family? Were they coming back soon? Maybe that was the reason Vinayak had mentioned this was a temporary solution. But did this mean he had a week, a month, a year before Vinayak sent him packing?

Kunal turned back to the window. A woman in a bright orange *saree* was bathing a child. The young boy, clad only in soap suds, ran around the muddy courtyard shrieking with joy while his mother chased him, laughing and admonishing him simultaneously. Round and round they ran; blurs of orange and brown. Did the boy know just how lucky he was? He touched the note in his shirt pocket, tucked close to his heart.

"Your turn," said Vinayak. He was dressed in clean clothes with wet, slicked-back hair. The fragrance of soap and toothpaste filled the room.

Kunal shuffled to the bathroom. Vinayak put a hand on his shoulder. "Wipe that gloomy look off your face. Things can't be all that bad on a sunny morning like this. And after breakfast you'll feel a lot better, I promise. So hurry up!"

On the way out they passed a dozen people lined up along the corridor and on the staircase, each armed with reading material and the inevitable mug of water. Vinayak caught Kunal's eye and winked as they hurried past. Kunal couldn't help but grin.

Sunshine Restaurant and Bakery was located the next street over from the *chawl*. A tantalizing aroma of freshly baked bread reeled them into the shabby yet clean eatery. Even at this early hour it was crowded.

"Hello-o-o, Vinayak! Who's this scrawny chicken with you? And what happened to his face?"

"Morning, Rustom." Vinayak greeted the massive proprietor, who looked more like a wrestler than a shopkeeper. He was perched on a stool at the entrance of the shop behind a white marble counter on which stood a cash register. Piled behind him were blackened trays filled with freshly baked crisp buns. Even as he greeted them, Rustom continued working, wrapping the buns at top speed in a piece of newspaper and handing them to customers. Though the line moved rapidly, it never seemed to shorten.

"Another tray of buns up front," hollered Rustom in the direction of the kitchen. "So, who is this?" he asked Vinayak again as they stood beside the counter waiting for a table.

"Kunal," said Vinayak. "He's staying with me for a few days. This *pehlwan* had a run-in with some ruffians, but nothing to worry about. He'll be all right in a week."

"Then bring him here every day," said Rustom. "We'll

fatten him up with our good food. At least he'll hold his own the next time. You'll have the usual?"

"Yes please," said Vinayak. "But Kunal may want to choose what he wants."

A waiter led them to a table and slapped a couple of menus, encased in cracked plastic, on the table. He sucked on a pencil stub, waiting for their order.

Kunal scanned the menu. There were so many mouthwatering choices; omelettes, scrambled eggs, mutton cutlets, *maska pao, kheema bun, baida roti*. The list seemed endless. He put it down. "I'll have what Vinayakji is having."

"*Chai* and *maska pao*, right?" said the boy, glancing at Vinayak and gathering up the menus. Vinayak nodded. The boy walked over to the pickup counter and placed the orders.

Kunal gazed around him. It was the first time he had ever sat at a table and ordered a meal. He felt grand as he leaned back in his chair and waited for his breakfast, which he would eat sitting down. Waiters smiled and joked with the customers as they delivered steaming plates of food. The aroma of fried eggs mingled with the fragrance of spicy omelettes and mutton cutlets. But the smell that stood out was of freshly baked bread with an underlying hint of sourness, which Kunal just could not get enough of. He sniffed so deeply and so often that Vinayak asked if he had a cold.

Occasionally, Rustom strode through the dining room, barely managing to squeeze his huge frame through the narrow gaps between the tables, greeting customers and even helping with clearing the dishes when it was extra busy — something Sethji would never have done.

"Who is this Rustom?" asked Kunal, his eyes steady on the huge proprietor. "And why does he talk in such a funny way?"

"He's a Parsee and a very good man," said Vinayak. "You'll get used to his way of speaking and his humour in no time at all."

"They all seem so happy here," said Kunal softly. "And Rustom is so different from Sethji." His stomach dropped at the mention of his former employer's name.

Vinayak leaned over and patted his shoulder. "That part of your life is over. You'll never go back there again, so stop worrying! It's Sunday and we both need a break. What would you like to do?"

"I'd like to see the financial district," said Kunal. The words jumped out of his mouth as if they'd been waiting there forever. The moment he uttered them, he knew it was the only thing he wanted to do today.

"Financial district it is," said Vinayak. "It's where most of the tiffins are delivered anyway. I'll take you to see the Queen's Necklace at Marine Drive, too. Have you seen it before?"

Kunal shook his head. He didn't know the Queen's Necklace was in Bombay, or why it was at Marine Drive. "Never been beyond Andheri Station and the area around the *dhaba*. That's where most of my deliveries took me."

Their breakfast arrived. The waiter plunked down their food and tea, left a chit of paper with "Rs. 5/-" written on it, and zipped away.

Kunal devoured the breakfast with his eyes first. Crisp brown buns, the size of his palm and oozing with golden butter, squatted on a plate giving off the most delicious fragrance. His stomach growled in delight. Vinayak was already biting into his bun, showering the table with crumbs. Kunal picked up the still-warm bread and took a large bite. *Oh yes*, he thought as he crunched up the mouthful, Rustom had named his restaurant well; this was definitely sunshine for the stomach.

Moments later both plates were empty. Kunal licked the butter from his fingers and sat back sipping the sweet lemony-minty tea.

"Hey, Kawas," Vinayak called out, reaching for his wallet. "Take care of this bill, will you?"

"I'd like to pay for my share, please," said Kunal. He dug out some coins from his pocket.

An expression of surprise and extreme sadness flickered on Vinayak's face and then it was gone.

"If you want to, Kunal, go ahead," said Vinayak. "You're your own master now."

Kunal loved the sound of those words.

They stepped into the street. A blast of muggy air laced with petrol fumes greeted them.

They walked at a leisurely pace while Vinayak pointed out various landmarks and interesting people. They stopped briefly to buy a *meetha paan*, which Vinayak stuffed into his mouth, and on they went.

Before long they were at Andheri Station. As soon as they

neared the entrance, a stream of passengers swept them along, like leaves in a strong current, and deposited them into the bowels of the station. Vendors pushed gaudy plastic combs, cheap watches, and newspapers under their noses. Beggars ran to and fro harassing commuters for money, blessing and cursing them in the same breath. The smell of rancid oil and burnt milk hung in the air. After buying tickets they pushed their way onto the platform.

A dirty yellow-and-brown train slid into the station. Some travellers squatted on the roof, very close to the electric wires. They didn't seem in the least worried as they sat clutching their ragged bundles, surveying the crowds below them with disdain. A few had boarded the train while it was still in motion, no doubt wanting to bag the vacant seats before the rest got on. As soon as the train squealed to a halt, a crowd of travellers surged towards the compartments trying to board, and were pushed back by an equally large crowd trying to get off. Tempers began to flare.

"*Abey*, *chutiye*, let me get off!"

"*Arre*, *gandu*, I have to get on. Can't miss this train."

Vinayak held Kunal's arm tightly as they joined the crowd and were pushed on board by hordes of bodies behind them. They squeezed into a corner and waited as people poured in.

The compartment was stuffed beyond capacity, and the stench was overpowering. Kunal identified Dabur Amla hair oil, a sickeningly sweet perfume, and rotting fish. The rest of the smells were indistinguishable but just as bad. He took shallow breaths, hoping the train ride wouldn't be too long. Already his *maska pao* was starting to climb up his throat. The train jerked its way towards their destination, but no one fell over. There wasn't room for it. Kunal could see nothing outside, so instead he focused on reading the various posters plastered along the interior of the train. There were advertisements for family planning, cooking classes, and how to cure piles. Kunal read them all, quite fascinated.

"Marine Lines!" said Vinayak. "To the door, quick." As the train slowed, Kunal and Vinayak fought their way through the densely packed crowds to the exit.

"Please let us through. Excuse me. Sorry. Excuse me. This is our station," Vinayak said as he steadily dragged Kunal towards the door. Kunal held his breath as his nose brushed past many a sweaty armpit.

The train stopped. They were ejected onto the platform along with a dozen other passengers. Kunal breathed deeply at last and smelled salt air. They walked the length of the platform, climbed a few stairs, and crossed a flyover high above the zipping cars. Even from here, Kunal could see the ocean spread out ahead; a dark grey mass of water mirroring a sky bulging with swollen clouds of rain.

Kunal leaped down the last few steps and dashed to the concrete parapet and the tetrapods. He stood there, his arms outstretched, staring at the expanse of water and the hazy row of buildings beyond, shrouded in smog.

"This is beautifu— ughh!"

A wave crashed against the parapet, drenching him. He shuddered and spat out a mouthful of salt water.

"This is Marine Drive, Kunal, and the first rule of

standing so close to the water is 'keep your mouth shut!'"
said Vinayak, laughing. He pointed to the buildings in the
distance. "That tall building is the Hotel Oberoi Towers.
And that one, with the circle on top, is the Air India Building.
He faced the opposite direction. "And if we go that way,
we can see the Gateway of India and the Taj Mahal Hotel.
So, which way do you want to go?"

"Financial district. That's all I'd like to see today," said
Kunal.

Vinayak looked at him curiously, but thankfully did not
ask any questions. Kunal volunteered no answers.

A cool wind swept up from the water. People hurried past,
clutching umbrellas. Vendors were busy unfurling scraps of
plastic and draping their food and wares in anticipation of
the imminent downpour. The sea turned darker, more violent.

They passed a vendor in a plastic cape and hat, selling
corn-on-the-cob. His small coal stove was perched on a
stand and protected from the wind by a blackened piece of
tin folded all around it. Two gunnysacks lay at his feet, one
filled with the raw vegetable and the other with husks. The
sweet smell of cooked corn perfumed the air.

"Want to try one?" asked Vinayak. "They're delicious."

Kunal shook his head as the first fat drops of rain
spattered the sidewalk. People scattered across the street
to the doorways of buildings, to bus stands, to any shelter
they could find. Vinayak grabbed his hand and they raced
to the nearest bus stand. They squeezed in with a dozen or
so people already standing there. Kunal watched the ocean
hiss and swell in front of him. The cluster of buildings

in the distance was almost obscured by the veil of water. Somewhere in that little corner of Bombay was where his mother worked. How was he going to find her?

As suddenly as the rain had started, it stopped. The sky cleared to a beaming blue and a light breeze tickled the surface of the sparkling water.

They resumed walking along the steaming sidewalk and reached the financial district a short while later. Vinayak wound his way through it, street by street, pointing out the buildings the alphanumeric codes on the tiffins represented. Kunal trailed Vinayak quietly trying to memorize all the new codes Vinayak was teaching him. It suddenly dawned on him, this area was vast: block upon block of space, buildings packed together as densely as the compartments on the local train during peak hours. It would be difficult — impossible — to find his mother here.

Vinayak gave him a gentle nudge. "You'd better pick up your chin. It's sweeping the sidewalk."

"What d'you mean?" said Kunal. He hated that Vinayak could read him so accurately.

"Most *dabbawallas* have six months of training to go through before they can make a delivery on their own. You'll have to worry about it only if you're accepted."

Kunal wanted to tell Vinayak why it was so important for him to be accepted; that his future depended on being able to find his mother. He opened his mouth and closed it again. Maybe some other time. He did not feel like explaining just yet. He stared at the dusty sidewalk. Had his mother ever walked here? Was he treading in her footsteps?

For lunch they went to a street vendor and bought a Bombay sandwich — layered with boiled potatoes, cucumbers, tomatoes, and green chutney.

As the day dribbled away, they turned once more towards the waterfront. Just before they emerged from the huddle of buildings, Vinayak said, "Close your eyes; I have a surprise for you."

Kunal promptly obeyed. Vinayak planted his hands on Kunal's shoulders and propelled him forward a few steps. "You can look now."

Kunal opened his eyes and his jaw dropped. Across the street at the water's edge, a row of glowing streetlights ran along the sidewalk, gently curving towards the horizon.

"That, Kunal, is called the Queen's Necklace," said Vinayak softly.

"I never knew streetlights could look so beautiful," Kunal said, unable to tear his gaze away from the graceful arc of lights against the backdrop of the blue-black ocean. "I could stand here forever."

Vinayak smiled. "I felt the same way when I first saw them. Still do."

They stood quietly, side by side, at the tip of Marine Drive, where the sidewalk ran out and the sea, speckled with golden lights, began. The gentle lapping of the water, the gradually deepening evening, and the smell of salt air filled Kunal's senses, pushing out the worry. There had to be a way to find his mother and, if he thought hard enough, it would come to him.

Kunal was quiet on the train ride back home.

"What's up?" said Vinayak. "Too much thinking is not good for one's health."

"How long can I stay with you?" asked Kunal.

"As long as it takes to get you on your feet," said Vinayak. "That is my promise to you."

As Kunal closed his eyes that night, the day played itself out again, ending with the breathtaking vision of the streetlights.

Chapter Ten

On Monday morning Kunal hurried to the station with Vinayak. The stand outside was almost full of cycles in various stages of being devoured by rust. The three-wheeled rickshaws, like giant black and yellow bugs, lined up patiently, awaiting passengers. Many a bare foot or arm stuck out of the vehicles as their drivers caught up on sleep.

Inside the station, chaos was starting to pick up. Announcements blared out at frequent intervals. Kunal got a whiff of fresh ink as they passed the newspaper kiosk, their displays screaming out yet another calamity in bold headlines. Food smells were starting to waft over the commuters: *batata-wadas*, *aloo-poori*, and *bhajiyas*. All mouth-wateringly delicious.

Vinayak barely glanced around him as he strode towards their regular spot to await his team members. Here they would all converge and re-sort the tiffins before starting the next leg of their journey. Vinayak had given Kunal a standard-size Gandhi cap that flopped over his ears and covered his eyes. "Just so the *dabbawallas* don't ask too many questions when they see you hanging around their tiffins," Vinayak had explained. Kunal didn't care that the cap didn't fit and that he probably looked ridiculous in it. For the first time he would actually see how this was done, maybe get the chance to sort tiffins!

Vinayak paced the small area, his eyes sweeping the length of the station.

"Don't you have to collect the tiffins from the *dhaba* anymore?" said Kunal.

"I've taken on other responsibilities and requested that the Association send someone else for those tiffins," said Vinayak. "I don't think it would be wise for either of us to show our faces to Sethji."

"Good idea," said Kunal. He could not help but think of Mrs. Seth. Hopefully she wasn't in worse shape than he was. He touched his face. It was still tender, though most of the swelling had subsided.

"Ahhh, here they come," said Vinayak. "Now, don't get in the way and don't touch anything. Just watch."

Dabbawallas poured into the station with their carriers, expertly manoeuvring around beggars, vendors, and commuters. Vinayak waited till they shed their heavy loads then immediately started sorting the tiffins, barely seeming to glance at the codes before putting them in the right carrier.

A young boy, slightly older than Kunal, raced up to them, the carrier seesawing dangerously on his head.

"Nikhil!" said Vinayak, looking up. "Good man, you're almost on time. Try to get here five minutes earlier tomorrow. Quick now, we must get your tiffins sorted. You get started and I'll send one of the men over to help."

84

Nikhil slid the carrier to the ground, almost dropping it on Kunal's foot. "Oops, sorry," he said, and flashed an apologetic smile. Kunal felt the boy's eyes linger on his face.

"No problem," said Kunal. He liked the look of this boy instantly. There was something about him that reminded Kunal of someone he knew. But who?

"I'll try, Vinayakji," said Nikhil. "I misjudged the time a bit today. Tomorrow will surely be better."

"It has to be," said Vinayak. "This means no talking with housewives even if they want you to stay and gossip. And if their tiffin is not ready, you don't wait for more than a minute. That'll teach them to be on time. But for your first attempt at doing the rounds on your own, you've done really well. *Shabaash!*"

Many *dabbawallas* joined in, praising Nikhil and patting the young boy on the back. Kunal watched with a twinge of jealousy. He had to get on the team; he had to be one of them — just till he found his mother. After that, if he was lucky, he wouldn't have to work full-time for a living. He might even go to school like a normal boy and make friends.

Kunal sidled up to Vinayak. "Can't I do just one tiffin?" he asked. "I think it's quite simple and I know so many of the codes already."

"Not now, Kunal. We're busy and I do not have the time to supervise you. We'll do this later, okay?" He strode between the carriers, his eyes scanning the tiffins.

Kunal moved closer to Nikhil. The young *dabbawalla* was slow to recognize the codes. When he was staring at a tiffin for a particularly long time, Kunal whispered to him,

"I think that's for the Air India building. It goes into that carrier bound for Churchgate."

Nikhil glanced around quickly. No one seemed to have noticed Kunal was helping him.

"Thanks," said Nikhil. "After a while these don't seem quite as confusing. What happened to your face?"

Kunal eyed him steadily for a moment. "I'll tell you some other time. For now let's just sort the tiffins, all right?"

"Okay!"

Together they finished distributing the tiffins from Nikhil's carrier. Kunal was glad he'd helped; he'd learned so many more codes. He was ready to do this, if only they'd give him a chance.

Nikhil raced to help someone else. Kunal wandered over to some carriers standing a little further away from the main hub of all the activity. There was no one close by, which meant they had already been sorted and were ready to go. No one was looking his way, either. Kunal picked up a box. The code *12 A 48* was inscribed in the centre of the lid. He wracked his brain. Which building was that?

The letters on it were blue, which meant this one would be picked up by the team delivering the blue-coded boxes. And what was that *E 14* at the side? He was sure Vinayak had told him what it stood for, back at the *dhaba*. If only he could remember.

"Oi! Put that down!" someone yelled.

Kunal started. The tiffin slid from his hands and crashed to the ground. A beefy *dabbawalla* strode up to Kunal, glared at him, bent down, and picked up the tiffin. He examined it cursorily and jammed it back into the carrier.

"How dare you touch these tiffins!" the *dabbawalla* said. "They're private property. I could get you arrested."

The station suddenly became unbearably hot as Kunal backed away from the *dabbawalla*, who stood glowering at him. He was large and well-built with burned skin and beady, black eyes. Everyone had stopped working. They were all staring at him. Questions bombarded Kunal from all directions.

"Who are you?"

"Where did you get that cap from?"

"What are doing near the tiffins?"

Kunal stood silently, staring at his feet.

"He's with me, Dubey," said Vinayak, coming up to them. "Friends, this is Kunal. He's staying with me for a while. He's shown an interest in becoming a *dabbawalla* and I guess he just couldn't wait to get started." Though he said this calmly enough, his mouth was rigid and his eyes unsmiling.

"I'm really sorry," Kunal mumbled, feeling his face turn hot. "I was just looking. I didn't mean any harm."

"You can look but you cannot touch!" said Dubey loudly. He faced Vinayak, a sneer on his face. "Are you a section leader or a joke?"

"That's enough!" said Vinayak, glaring at Dubey. "It was a mistake and it won't happen again. You watch your mouth with your superior or I'll report you to the management!"

Dubey returned Vinayak's glare and walked back to his own team. Kunal took a step towards Vinayak, who frowned and turned away.

"Don't feel too bad," someone whispered. It was Nikhil. "Dubey's like that with everyone, so we call him *Goo-bay*."

Kunal's lips twitched at the nickname, which so accurately described Dubey's crabby nature. Nikhil winked as he struggled to balance the carrier on his head. "I'm only doing the first part of the deliveries today," he called out as he hurried away. "I'll see you back at the office in an hour."

Then Kunal was all alone in the crowd. His eyes roved over the carriers littering a corner of the station, at the *dabbawalla*s as they readied themselves for the approaching train, knowing exactly what to do and how to do it. The longing to belong crushed him.

The ten a.m. train slid into the station in a mustard-coloured blur. The *dabbawallas* ran alongside, carriers balanced expertly on their heads, each picking a compartment to board as soon as the train came to a halt. Commuters ran alongside, too, adding to the chaos. Kunal stared at the impossibly crowded platform. How would the commuters get off? How would the *dabbawallas* get on? There didn't seem to be enough room for them all. And still more came, crossing in front of the slowing train and leaping onto the platform; men, women, even children.

Just as the train ground to a complete stop, a scuffle broke out; two *dabbawallas* were trying to board the same compartment.

"Dubey's men are at it again," muttered Vinayak to no one in particular. "Just as bad as their leader."

Commuters swirled near the entrances of the train's compartments. Vendors weaved in and out of the dense crowds, pushing their wares under people's noses or holding them up for the inspection of those already seated inside. They looked like caged animals, peering out through the barred windows. Vinayak and Dubey reached their men at the same time and broke up the fight. Vinayak's man ran off to board another compartment and the train rattled off. The tiffins were on their way, on time as always.

"Let's go," said Vinayak. He strode past Kunal, not looking at him.

"You're still mad at me, aren't you?" said Kunal.

Vinayak stopped and turned to face him. "What do you think? You disobey me on the very first day I bring you here, give the meanest man in my section a chance to publicly humiliate me, and then you ask silly questions!"

This was the very first time Kunal had ever received a tongue-lashing from Vinayak. It felt a lot worse than Sethji's yelling. Kunal whirled and ran out of the station.

"Kunal, come back here!"

Ignoring Vinayak, Kunal ran through the courtyard, dodging rickshaws, beggars, and a stray cow chewing its cud. He reached the main road. He heard Vinayak running after him, calling out. Without a second thought, Kunal plunged into the slow-moving traffic. A scooter, piled high with an entire family, screeched to a halt inches away from him.

"*Saala Pagal!*" the man yelled. "Can't you watch where you're going? You could have got us all killed!" The scooter swayed precariously as the driver's wife and four kids hung on for dear life. "Idiot!" he spat out for good measure.

"Sorry," mumbled Kunal, wiping the sweat from his face.

His heart was racing and he felt sick.

The traffic continued to flow on either side of them. The man yelled a bit more, gunned the engine, and sped away, his family clinging to various parts of his anatomy.

Vinayak had caught up to him by now, berating him and crying all at once. He shook Kunal by the shoulders, then hugged him. Kunal stared at him; had he traded in Sethji's brutality for Vinayak's strangeness?

"I'm sorry," was all Kunal could say.

Vinayak wiped his face on the sleeve of his *kurta* and dragged Kunal to the sidewalk amid a flurry of honks and curses.

"I'm sorry too," said Vinayak. "Let's sit down for a moment. I need to talk to you."

Kunal nodded. He had to understand what was going on and the reason for this old man's bizarre behaviour moments ago. He followed Vinayak towards some food stalls set up under the shade of a dusty banyan tree. One of the vendors was selling watermelon juice. The large aluminum tub filled with juicy chunks of red fruit and ice cubes looked very inviting.

"Just what we both need to cool down," said Vinayak. He ordered two glasses and they sat under the shade of the tree to enjoy them.

Kunal watched the scooters and rickshaws zoom past, weaving in and out of the trucks and buses with reckless abandon. Vinayak was quiet.

"Why were you so upset, Vinayakji?"

"This traffic is so dangerous," said Vinayak. "It reminds

me of something I'd rather not talk about right now." His voice broke.

"You've lost someone, haven't you?" asked Kunal. "When you think no one is watching, you always look sad. Why won't you tell me? Let *me* help you for a change?"

Vinayak looked steadily into Kunal's eyes for a long moment, but did not answer. His fingers played with his wedding ring, twisting it around and around.

Maybe it was his wife he'd lost. That would explain why he was constantly playing with his wedding ring and the fact that the kitchen in his room was no longer in use. Kunal decided not to probe further.

Vinayak took a sip of the sherbet. "Why did you touch the tiffins when I told you not to?"

"I wanted to see if I could remember all the codes, that's all. If I could prove that I know how to read them, the Association might hire me as a *dabbawalla* sooner."

"Kunal, reading the codes is only part of the job. But why now, what's the hurry?"

"To find my mother," said Kunal.

"Your mother? But I thought you were ..."

"An orphan," said Kunal. It was a small word, but a word that was as painful as a sliver in a finger. "Yes, I thought so too until Mrs. Seth told me the truth just before I left the *dhaba*."

"So, that's why you went back? To get the names of your parents?"

Kunal stared into the depths of the remaining juice in his glass. "Yes." He plunked the glass on the ground suddenly and grabbed Vinayak's arm. "Mrs. Seth gave me the note my mother wrote when she left me at the *dhaba*. I don't know where she is but I know her name. I have to find her! Something must have happened to stop her from coming back for me. I just know it. You'll help me find her, won't you?" Seeing the closeness of the *dabbawallas* this morning made him all the more determined to find his own family. As soon as possible. Kunal didn't want to waste a single minute.

Vinayak sighed deeply. "We're late. It's time we made our way to the head office. I'll ask the management about you today."

"Do I stand a chance of being accepted?" Kunal asked.

"I really do not have the answer to that," said Vinayak, "but we'll find out soon enough."

It was much later that Kunal realized Vinayak had not answered his other question: the one about helping him find his mother.

The head office of the Dabbawalla Association was a twenty minute walk from the station on the first floor of a dilapidated structure that seemed to be standing only because it was propped up by buildings on either side. They climbed a gloomy wooden staircase lit by low-watt bulbs at irregular intervals. The dirty white wall running alongside was adorned with *paan* spatters. It seemed as if someone had celebrated *Holi* on the staircase with only one colour: red.

The room was filled with *dabbawallas* and everyone was talking amongst themselves. Kunal heard snatches of conversation: discussions about wages, train schedules, and starting a petition to have their own compartment in trains at peak delivery times. The stench of sweat, *beedis*, and *paan* thickened the stagnant air in the room.

Kunal positioned himself near a window trying to gulp in a lungful of clean air. Vinayak greeted many men and listened to the discussions quietly. When he did offer an opinion, everyone paid attention and no one interrupted. A few moments later, a tiny man with thick glasses shuffled into the room. He looked so ancient, Kunal wondered how he had the energy to walk.

"That's the head of the Association — Hari," said Vinayak. "He's the one we need permission from."

Hari clapped his hands once and the murmur died down immediately. He settled himself at a round table flanked by two men; one who looked like a shrivelled prune and a younger man with salt-and-pepper hair.

"Who are the other two?" said Kunal.

"The older man is Suhas and the greying one is Param," whispered Vinayak. "Those three make up the senior management of the Association."

Kunal nodded, staring at them. They were the first steps to finding his mother. The trio looked around the room, missing nothing. He felt their eyes rest on him for a few seconds before moving on.

"What's on the agenda today?" asked Hari. His voice sounded like the crackling of old newspaper.

"Can we raise the monthly delivery fee?" someone asked. "These days, a hundred rupees per month is just not enough to survive on. Prices of everything have gone through the roof."

"No, we can't," replied Param. "We'll lose a lot of customers. There's a private company that has started a similar service. They are waiting for the first opportunity to steal our customers and the low price we charge is to our advantage."

"Many customers are using the tiffin as a message service," the same *dabbawalla* said. "There are at least three women on my route who put notes in their tiffins; sometimes a grocery list or other instructions for their husbands. They save a few rupees on the phone call they'd have to make otherwise. Surely they wouldn't mind paying a little extra for that convenience?"

Kunal's ears perked up. *A message in a tiffin?* "It's their box," said Suhas. "They can put whatever they like in it, be it food or a note. As long as the weight is not beyond normal, we will deliver it — on time! Remember our motto: *Work is Worship.*"

Nikhil raised his hand slowly. All eyes swivelled to him and he turned crimson.

"Yes?" said Hari in a kind voice. "Our youngest member has something to say?"

"There's a young woman on my route," said Nikhil in a breathless voice, "who sends love notes to her boyfriend without her mother's knowledge. She often waits for me at the street corner and I have to unload the tiffin so she can slip it in. She's so polite, I really don't mind, but should I allow it?"

Kunal was reminded of his mother, who had done the same thing. Except that her love story had not ended happily. "Not in love with her too, are you?" someone teased, and Nikhil protested vehemently amid hoots and whistles.

Param rapped on the table and the noise died down again. "As long as it does not delay you, it's all right. But if it does, you have to say no."

Kunal was lost in thought. How wonderful it would be to open his tiffin, unfold a *chapati*, and see a note lying there. A note from someone who loved him. He wondered how his father must have felt receiving the love notes from his mother, writing a reply, and sending it back.

That was it!

He thought his heart would burst with joy. He wanted to yell it out loud: *he knew exactly how to search for his mother*. He clapped his hand on his mouth and glanced at Vinayak, but the old man did not look his way.

He would write as many notes as possible and stuff them into the thousands of tiffins that were delivered daily in the financial district. One of them was bound to reach the right Anahita Patel. But first he had to become one of them and only then the *dabbawallas* would listen to him. *Speak up, Vinayak*, he prayed silently. *Ask them about me. Now.*

Vinayak spoke up, almost as if he had heard Kunal's fervent prayer. "I have a request," he said, looking at the seniors.

"Go ahead, Vinayak."

"I'd like to ask that this boy, Kunal," said Vinayak, touching him lightly on the shoulder, "be allowed to become a *dabbawalla*. He is young but an honest and hard worker. I can personally vouch for that. His training will be my responsibility. Will the Association give me permission to do so?"

Not even a murmur disturbed the still air in the room.

"Vinayak," said Hari, "you know that we only induct members from our own community. Who is this boy's family? Is he a *Maharashtrian*?"

"How does that matter?" a shrill voice said. All eyes focused on Kunal and he realized the voice had been his. He thought he would burst into flames.

Hari was looking at him with a stern expression. Suhas's mouth puckered up some more, and Param ran his fingers through his hair impatiently. No one said a word.

"I'm sorry," said Kunal, "but why is that important? I'm a hard worker. I've been delivering food for years at a *dhaba* and I can learn quickly. Are all the members from your community excellent workers? Has no one let you down? Ever?"

The silence took on a strained quality.

"That is not your place to question and it's none of your business," said Hari. He looked as if he'd just bitten into a lemon. "You cannot join us till we know your family background, and even then it is a matter subject to discussion. We can't let just anybody become a *dabbawalla*; we have a reputation to protect."

"And that's why I'm asking for this job: so I can find my family — my mother," said Kunal. "Please help me. Say yes!"

"That's enough," said Hari. "This is no place for children

who like throwing tantrums. Vinayak, from now on you will come alone to the meetings. If I want drama, I can watch a movie. The meeting is over."

Kunal stared at the seniors as they filed out of the room. It emptied rapidly once they were gone. Some stayed behind to talk to Vinayak. Nikhil stopped for a moment and squeezed Kunal's shoulder. Then he too was gone.

Kunal's euphoria from a few moments ago evaporated. He'd never be able to send those notes and find his mother. He was doomed to be an orphan for the rest of his life. The unfairness of it all was like a boulder on his chest. He marched out of the room, not bothering to wait for Vinayak.

Chapter Eleven

The comfortable aromas of food enveloped Kunal in their warm embrace as he sat with Vinayak at a table in Sunshine, waiting for their dinner.

"Can you please stop looking as if someone just died?" said Vinayak.

"I was so sure they would let me join," said Kunal. "How could they be so heartless?"

"But I did tell you it was unlikely, no?" said Vinayak. "Surely it didn't come as a complete surprise."

Kunal shrugged. "So now what? How do I earn a living? I can't live forever on what Mrs. Seth gave me and I don't want to be a burden on you."

"Don't ever say that again," said Vinayak quietly. "Besides, I've already made arrangements to get you a job." He winked at Kunal, but didn't elaborate.

"What is it?" asked Kunal, not the least bit happy with the news. He wanted to be a *dabbawalla*. He could think of no other way to find his mother.

"Uh-uh," said Vinayak, shaking his head and smiling. "You'll have to wait just a little bit longer."

"Tell me now!" said Kunal. "Mrs. Seth was always hiding things from me; she hid the most important information of all. Why do people do that?"

"There you go, being dramatic again," said Vinayak. "Calm down, I only wanted to give you a nice surprise. I was going to tell you after dinner."

Before Kunal could ask more questions, their food arrived and along with it, the massive proprietor. He lowered his bulk into a chair, which groaned in protest. Fragrant steam rose from mutton cutlets sandwiched in a bun. Kunal looked at it without much appetite.

"So," said Rustom, "this is the boy you were talking about. Kunal, isn't it?"

Vinayak nodded as he pushed a plate towards Kunal and started on his own meal.

Rustom's large hand shot out suddenly and he squeezed Kunal's biceps. "He doesn't look like he can last one hour on the job," he said, "let alone a whole day."

"I've seen him work at the *dhaba*, which supplied my customers' tiffin lunches," said Vinayak through a mouthful of food. "He's a fast worker and very good. And he can last a whole day, maybe more! Ummm, this cutlet is good, Rustom."

"What job?" asked Kunal, looking from one to the other.

"Hmmm," said Rustom. "Not too bright, either." But there was a twinkle in his eye.

Vinayak put down his bun and swallowed the mouthful. "I've asked Rustom to hire you. Think you can do it?"

"I used to work a ten-hour shift," said Kunal. "I can do

it." He watched Rustom carefully, his stomach in knots. Till this afternoon he had been jobless and now he had the chance to get a decent job, to earn a livelihood and still carry out his plan.

"Let's see if you're up to it," said Rustom, thumping the table with his palm. "I'm off tomorrow so you can start the day after."

"Seriously?" asked Kunal. He looked from Vinayak to Rustom. "You mean that?"

"Oh yes, I do," said the proprietor. "One more thing: I look after my boys and feed them well, but I work them hard."

"I won't let you down," said Kunal.

"Good!" said Rustom. "You start work at seven sharp in the morning. I'll pay you fifty rupees a month. You work six days a week and you get one weekday off. We all work Saturdays and Sundays since they're the busiest. If you fall sick, I take it out of your pay. Any questions?"

"Yes," said Kunal.

"I was just being polite, *gadhera*," said Rustom, getting to his feet. "Make it quick."

"Can I work the afternoon shift instead of the morning?" said Kunal.

"Why?"

"I'd like to go with Vinayakji to the station every morning. You know, just to help out with the tiffins. I hope you don't mind," Kunal said, glancing at Vinayak.

Vinayak's face was unreadable but he gave a brief nod. "I'm okay with it if your new employer is."

"All right then," said Rustom. "Afternoon shift it is. Come in at noon and work till midnight. Got it?"

"Thank you," said Kunal. "Er ... one last thing: what's a *gadhera*?"

"You'll find out soon enough," Rustom called over his shoulder. He hurried to his usual spot behind the counter where customers were starting to line up.

Vinayak was chomping on the last of his bun thoughtfully.

"Thank you, Vinayakji."

"It's the least I could do," said Vinayak. "Plus, it's a job you know well, so it shouldn't be a problem. Right?"

"But how will I search for my mother if I can't be a *dabbawalla*? Just when I've figured out exactly how to find her, I can't!"

Vinayak's face tightened. He said nothing.

"You will help me look for her," said Kunal, quietly. "Won't you?"

"No."

The bun slid out of Kunal's hands. "How can you say that? You know what this means to me. Of all people, I thought you were my friend, and would be willing to help."

"Going down this path will only cause pain. I refuse to be a part of it."

Kunal stared at Vinayak, unable to believe his ears. *My mother is alive. I have family. I'm not an orphan!* How could he find the right words to describe just how important this was to him? And why should he have to?

Vinayak was looking at him steadily almost as if he'd read his mind. "You know her name and you know she left you with Mrs. Seth and did not come back. That doesn't change anything."

"Maybe something happened that made it impossible for her to come back," said Kunal. "Her note said she loved me. That she'd be back in a week."

"May I read it?" said Vinayak.

Kunal took a deep breath. He extracted the precious piece of paper from his pocket and wordlessly handed it over. Vinayak read the note, folded it, and handed it back to him.

"How old are you?" said Vinayak quietly.

"Twelve."

"Think about it for a moment. For twelve years your mother knew where you were because she left you there. Right?"

Kunal nodded. The mouthful he had just swallowed stuck in his throat.

"All this while she did not come to get you. And now you think that once you find her, she'll welcome you with open arms? No, she won't."

Kunal stared at Vinayak wishing he could break something and see it shatter into a million pieces. Why did Vinayak have to say stupid things like this? He was wrong, so very wrong. Kunal struggled to think clearly, but his mind had shut down. All he heard were Vinayak's words: *No, she won't.*

"It's late. If you're not going to finish your bun then we'd better go," said Vinayak. He put some money on the table.

They rose and walked out of the restaurant. Vinayak waved goodbye to Rustom. Kunal could barely meet his eye.

Outside, the air crackled with electricity. Thunderclouds plodded overhead, prodded on by flashes of lighting.

"More rain tomorrow," said Vinayak with a deep sigh. "When all that water up there is down on the streets, you'll be dry and warm in Sunshine while my boys will be out in the floods delivering tiffins. You'll be happy you didn't get the job."

Kunal glanced up into the ominous face of the sky. He would have cheerfully delivered tiffins in a typhoon in order to meet the woman who had brought him into the world. And ask her why she had abandoned him.

It rained all night. The roads had disappeared under filthy brown water pockmarked with floating debris and dead rats. Buses and cars traversed the flooded roads, splashing the already soaked pedestrians. Everything in sight dripped.

And still it rained.

Kunal sloshed through knee-deep water stinking of raw sewage and entered Andheri Station, drenched from head to toe. Vinayak, who had used the only umbrella he possessed, was scarcely dryer. They stood just inside the entrance and squeezed the water from their clothes. The staccato drumbeat of rain on the station's tin roof was unusually loud.

"Today will be quite an interesting day," said Vinayak. He closed the umbrella and propped it against a wall. "It will be a challenge to deliver the tiffins on time."

"Will they manage?" asked Kunal, slicking back his hair, feeling a rivulet of cold water trickle down his neck. "With all this rain?"

"Most are old hands at it. A couple of the younger ones, probably Nikhil, may have difficulty. We'll see how it goes. Now stay out of the way today. I really can't handle any distractions."

Kunal decided to do exactly as he was told. There was enough to keep him interested. Commuters hurried into the station, wiping their streaming faces with sodden handkerchiefs. The *chai-walla* was doing roaring business as were the *samosa* and *vada* sellers. The fragrances of the savoury fried foods wafted his way, making his mouth water.

Clean, shiny trains rattled in and out of the station. There were the usual mad dashes on slick asphalt at the edge of the station with the inevitable tumbles, red-faced embarrassment, and helping hands. Kunal watched them, all the while thinking, might his mother be on some platform, waiting for the train? Or would she be driving to work in a fancy car?

*Dabbawalla*s were starting to pour in, laughing and swearing in the same breath. They had taken the weather in their stride and seemed all the more efficient as they sorted the boxes at top speed and then raced to help the next dripping fellow worker.

"Oi, Moray," said Vinayak to a *dabbawalla* who'd just come in. "Where's Nikhil?"

Moray lowered the carrier to the floor and wiped his face. His white *kurta* pyjama was plastered to his body, and splattered with mud.

"I haven't seen him yet," said Moray.

"This is his first monsoon collecting the tiffins on his

own," said Vinayak. "I hope he had the sense to start the collection early. His route has eight boxes that have to be redistributed. The train schedules are going to be a mess today."

"He'll make it," Moray replied. "We still have ten minutes before our train comes in."

Vinayak checked his watch and started sorting the tiffins in Moray's carrier while the *dabbawalla* attempted to wring the water out of his clothes. Kunal moved closer.

"Kunal, isn't it?" said Moray, noticing him for the first time.

"Yes."

"Sure is bad out there." Moray jerked his head towards the silver sheet of water cascading off the station's roof and onto the tracks. "This weather tests the mettle of even the best *dabbawalla*. It's a challenge to deliver the food hot, and on time!"

"Have you lost any tiffins?" asked Kunal. "It's a really bad thing to happen, right?'

"Right," said Moray. "No one likes to be the one to mar our record of nearly one hundred percent accuracy, but sometimes accidents do happen. Luckily, I've never lost a tiffin." He finished wiping himself and knelt beside Vinayak to help with the sorting. "But an almost fatal incident occurred last year. An open manhole just outside Charni Road Station was covered up by the flood waters. The *dabbawalla* wading through chest-deep water obviously didn't see it, and walked straight into it. He would have been swept away into the sewers if it had not been for the carrier. It saved his life!"

"I remember that one," said Vinayak. He looked up momentarily. "It was Suresh, wasn't it?"

"Yes," said Moray. "The tiffins fell off, but the carrier landed across the manhole and gave him something to hold on to. Passersby who had seen him go down immediately helped him out. He collected all the tiffins and went about the delivery as he'd been trained. Then he came back to the office and cried like a baby. Amazing boy!"

Kunal listened to the story, his eyes not leaving Moray's face. The *dabbawallas* took their job seriously, upholding the tradition and their impeccable track record as a team. Once again something twisted inside him. They were all so close, like a family. They even had stories they could recount. They belonged, whereas he had a past he wanted to forget, and belonged to no one.

Vinayak stood up. "Nikhil's late."

Automatically, Kunal's eyes went to the clock on the station wall; a white-faced dial with strict black numbers and stiff hands.

Five minutes to ten.

A *dabbawalla* came up to them. "The tracks are starting to get flooded," he said. "If it gets too bad, the next train will be delayed and so will the tiffins. We'd better make sure all of us are on this one. Who's missing?"

Vinayak did not answer. Instead he paced the floor, took off his Gandhi cap, smoothed the band and put it back on. He looked at the clock again.

"Nikhil," said Kunal, when he saw that the *dabbawalla*

was still waiting for an answer.

The *dabbawalla* nodded and looked up at the clock. Kunal glanced up too.

Four minutes to ten.

The *dabbawallas* stood up in readiness. Vinayak gave last minute instructions. Two of them were to help sort Nikhil's carrier as soon as he came in. He glanced at the entrance for what seemed like the hundredth time. So did Kunal.

Three minutes to ten.

The commuters surged forward. A nasal voice announced the arrival of the ten a.m. train to Churchgate. Dubey appeared out of the crowd.

"I have two boxes missing from one of your team members, bound for Bandra. Where the hell are they?"

"They'll be here," said Vinayak in a calm voice. "We're waiting for Nikhil. It's his first time collecting the tiffins in such heavy rain, but I'm confident he'll make it."

"Even if he does, you'll never sort them by the time the train comes in. You should have had a senior take over the route today," said Dubey. "Not a very smart section leader, are you?"

The tan on Vinayak's face deepened. He had just opened his mouth when someone yelled, "There he is! Nikhil's arrived!"

All heads swivelled to the entrance. A carrier was moving towards them slowly through the milling crowds. Everyone's eyes were glued to it.

The hands of the clock ticked into position and it started chiming out the hours.

The sound seemed to galvanize Nikhil. He sped through the crowds towards the edge of the platform where there were fewer people.

"Move, MOVE!" Kunal heard him yell as he sprinted towards them.

Commuters jumped out of the way of this determined young boy with his unwieldy carrier who neither slowed nor swerved for anyone.

"*Shabaash*," yelled Vinayak. "Faster. We can make it yet."

Nikhil was but a few feet away from them when he slipped on the slick asphalt. The carrier jumped out of his hands, teetered at the edge of the platform and went over.

"NO!" shrieked Nikhil, lunging for it. He missed and it landed with a crash on the tracks, scattering tiffins like silver confetti.

The commuters crowded forward, watching the spectacle. The *dabbawallas* and Kunal raced as one towards Nikhil. He stared at them for a moment, then at his tiffins. Then he jumped.

"You idiot, come back up now!" roared Vinayak. He skidded to a halt at the edge of the platform, got down on all fours and reached out for Nikhil, who was flinging the tiffins up onto the platform. The boy skilfully avoided Vinayak's attempt to grab him as he hopped over the shining tracks gathering the boxes.

"Come up NOW!" said Vinayak. "If I have to come down, I'll thrash you so hard you won't be able to use your backside for a month."

"I can't spoil our record!" yelled Nikhil. "I can't let you

down." His voice was almost lost in the drumbeat of the rain.

Kunal looked at Nikhil's crazed face, streaming with rain as he feverishly worked to retrieve all the boxes. The heavy downpour made everything soft and hazy. Nikhil wiped his eyes frequently, searching for the remaining tiffins and keeping a lookout for the train. And then he suddenly realized: Nikhil reminded him of Lalan. And he looked just as scared as Lalan had the evening he'd been brutally beaten.

"Are you insane, Vinayak?" said Dubey. "Get that boy up here or you'll be the first section leader in history to lose a life instead of a tiffin."

Vinayak turned pale. He dropped to his knees and Kunal knew exactly what he was about to do.

"I'll get him back," said Kunal. Before he could change his mind or anyone could stop him, Kunal jumped onto the tracks.

"NO!" said Vinayak. "Not you too."

"Nikhil," said Kunal, trying to shut out the instructions that the *dabbawallas* and commuters were yelling out to them. "Help me with the carrier first. Hurry!"

They picked up the carrier and handed it to the waiting *dabbawallas*.

"The train's coming!" someone called out. "Get off the tracks."

Kunal heard the mournful horn. The vibrations under his feet intensified.

"It's almost here," yelled Kunal.

Nikhil froze, staring up the track. The clattering of the wheels was deafeningly loud now. The snub-nosed face of the train was getting clearer through the haze of rain and it was coming fast.

"Move!" yelled Kunal. "We can do it."

Together they managed to retrieve the last two tiffins and fling them onto the platform.

"Leave the tiffins!"

"Come on, up!"

Kunal pushed Nikhil up first. A dozen waiting hands pulled him to safety.

"Kunal, hurry up and take my hand," Vinayak screamed, leaning out as far as he could.

Kunal reached out for Vinayak's outstretched hand when a flash of silver caught his eye. A lone tiffin lay on a wooden sleeper of the track furthest away from them. His heart thumped.

"We missed one!" said Kunal, pointing. "There!"

"Leave it," Vinayak pleaded. He leaned further out to grab Kunal. "It doesn't matter!"

But it did matter. Dubey stood at the platform's edge, smirking. Ignoring Vinayak's outstretched hand, Kunal whirled around and raced for the tiffin. The train thundered towards him. Kunal jumped and cleared the track seconds before the train slid past, obscuring Vinayak and the *dabbawallas* from view.

Kunal snatched up the last tiffin triumphantly. Vinayak's reputation and their record remained unmarred. Dubey could go to hell. He clutched the tiffin to his chest, wanting to laugh, wishing the others could see him. He hopped along the wooden sleepers towards the steps of the platform on the other side. He would take the bridge across and this tiffin could go in the next train.

Vibrations under his feet again. Staccato beat of steel on steel. Close and coming closer. He looked up, his heart pounding.

The brown and yellow face of a train heading in the opposite direction was almost upon him. Through the glass window in front of the train he caught sight of the driver's horrified face.

Once more he jumped.

Chapter Twelve

Kunal landed with a thud in the narrow corridor between the two train tracks. Gravel and pebbles dug into his knees while the unceasing rain tattooed his back. The screeching of wheels on metal filled his ears as the trains swept off in opposite directions. Crouching low, he hugged the tiffin to his chest, praying he wouldn't be sucked under. The wind pulled at his clothes as the trains picked up speed. Kunal was almost flat on the ground, his face pressed to the gravel, breathing in the stench of urine, feces, and hot metal. The wind lessened and the vibrations died away and still he crouched. He hadn't the strength to sit up or even look around.

Strong arms pulled him to his feet. He opened his eyes. Two *dabbawallas* were on the track. They dragged him towards the platform. More hands reached out and pulled him up and still he did not let go off the tiffin — it seemed glued to his fingers.

The next moment Nikhil lunged at him and hugged him tight. "Thank you, *thank you*! You're the bravest person I have ever met."

"Anyone would have done the same," said Kunal. His voice sounded odd in his ears; high-pitched and shaky. But the truth was that no one else had jumped onto the tracks. He had. Nikhil grinned at him and Kunal managed a smile. It was just starting to sink in: he'd saved the last tiffin and the *dabbawallas*' record, single-handedly.

"I'd better take that tiffin now," said Nikhil. "I'll catch the next train. I think we'll still be able to deliver it without too much of a delay, thanks to you."

Kunal handed it over and Nikhil scampered off. He turned and came face to face with Vinayak. The smile died on his lips. Vinayak's face was bloodless. His blazing eyes still held vestiges of terror. The old man shook Kunal till his teeth rattled. "You stupid boy! That was the silliest and most dangerous thing I have ever seen in my life! Don't you ever stop to think before you act?" He swivelled on his heel and walked away.

Kunal stared at the *dabbawallas* who had stayed behind to help him. The rest had already boarded the ten a.m. train and were on their way to the city centre. "What did I do wrong? I helped Nikhil and saved your record and he's angry at me for that? Has he gone mad?"

"That was a brave thing to do, but really, the lives of our people are more important than our record," one of them replied. "If anything had happened to you, Vinayak would never have forgiven himself. He's already lost too much. I thought you knew that."

Then Kunal remembered Vinayak's reaction when he had run into the street a couple of days ago. The old man had lost someone dear to him — something Kunal suspected but it had completely slipped his mind. What agony Vinayak must have gone through seeing him on the tracks.

He dropped to his knees, shivering and nauseous, as the enormity of what he had done sunk in. So many things could have gone wrong, and Vinayak would have been in greater trouble. A hot wave rose within him. He opened his mouth and a torrent of vomit shot out. Only when all of his breakfast was on the platform did he sit back. Someone handed him a glass of water. He took a sip and almost gagged.

"It's all right, you're safe," said the voice he had been aching to hear.

Vinayak squatted beside him, rubbing his back. "Are you okay now or do you want to lie down?"

"I'm sorry, so very sorry," said Kunal. He gazed into Vinayak's eyes. They had lost their livid look.

"Let's go back to the head office," said Vinayak. "The seniors will want a report on this."

"You've forgiven me, haven't you?" said Kunal as they walked out the station.

Vinayak was silent for a moment. "Yes," he said. "I know you acted with the best of intentions. None of the men had the courage to do what you did. But I couldn't help thinking of someone else ... someone I loved dearly and lost."

They were almost at the entrance. Vinayak stopped suddenly and clutched his chest. A sheen of sweat covered his forehead.

"Are you all right?" asked Kunal. "Do you want to sit

down?" The old man's face looked as grey as the sky outside and Kunal felt sick just watching him.

Vinayak leaned against a wall. He closed his eyes and breathed deeply. Slowly, colour suffused his face and he opened them again. "Just had a bit of a shock," he said. "I'm fine now."

"Who were you reminded of?" asked Kunal. He wanted to know ... he had to know.

Vinayak did not answer. Avoiding Kunal's eyes, he straightened up and wiped his forehead with a trembling hand.

"Why won't you tell me?" said Kunal. "Am I not like a son to you?"

Vinayak looked at Kunal then, his eyes wet. "That is why I was so afraid for you ... for me, if I lost you. But now is not the time to talk about this. I'll tell you when we are both ready."

Kunal tried to hug Vinayak. "I'm so sorry."

Vinayak held him at arm's length. "Just stop and think before you act. All right? And please, don't ever jump onto train tracks again."

Kunal nodded. "As long as no one drops tiffins on the tracks, I won't," he replied.

A ghost of a smile flitted across Vinayak's face.

As soon as they entered the head office, the senior *dabbawallas* crowded round Kunal. They patted his back, tousled his hair, and a couple of them clasped his hands in their callused ones and pumped hard.

"That was amazing!"

"No one has ever shown this kind of commitment or bravery before."

"Or this kind of stupidity," someone piped in. Kunal was sure that had been Dubey.

"Our track record of ninety-nine percent accuracy remains unmarred, for now!"

"*Shabaash*."

Kunal smiled and thanked each person. The senior members came up to him. Hari looked him in the eye.

"That was a good thing you did for us all," he said. "Though, from what I hear, it could have been a disaster. The Association would rather lose a tiffin than a life. Remember that the next time you feel the need to act like Amitabh Bachchan."

"I'm sorry, Hariji," said Kunal. "But I couldn't think of anything but saving the tiffins. Doesn't rule twenty-three of the *dabbawalla* code state that no customer shall go hungry?"

Hari stared at him for a long minute. "I can see that you have an excellent work ethic and a keen interest in being one of us."

He turned to Suhas and Param, who were flanking him, and whispered something. They nodded and he turned back.

"We have decided to grant your wish."

Kunal gaped at Hari, then at Vinayak.

"You wanted to be a *dabbawalla*," said Hari. "You have our permission. You can start with us tomorrow."

Loud cheering filled the room.

Kunal was quiet. At last, the words he had longed to

hear. He would become a *dabbawalla*, though it would take almost six months of training before he could deliver the tiffins on his own. That was too long a time to wait for what he had to do right now.

The senior *dabbawalla* was staring at him perplexed. "Aren't you happy? Isn't that what you asked for the last time we saw you?"

Kunal took a deep breath. "There's something I want even more."

Only the whirring of the fan disturbed the silence in the room.

"I want your help to find my mother."

Chapter Thirteen

"What?" said Hari. For a moment he almost looked sorry that he had started this conversation. He glanced at his colleagues who had moved closer.

"How do you propose we do that?" asked Param.

Kunal glanced at Vinayak, who hadn't said a word. His eyes seemed to have sunk deeper into their sockets and the lines on his face were more prominent than ever. It was clear Vinayak hated this idea. But now was his chance, maybe his only chance to find his family and belong to someone.

"The other day I heard you all talking about customers putting notes in their tiffins," said Kunal. He was so excited that the words spilled out of his mouth. "I'd like to send out notes addressed to my mother in all the tiffins delivered to the financial district. That's where she works. One of those notes will surely reach her. I'll have my family again and then ... then ... er ... I can join you." His voice trailed off. Once he had found her, he hoped he wouldn't need to continue working full-time; that he might have time to go to school like other boys his age.

"Out of the question," said Hari. A deep scowl replaced

his normally benign expression. "We can't jeopardize the integrity of our service just to find your mother. The customers will be annoyed."

His words deflated the bubble of joy within Kunal. "But you said you wanted to repay me. Well, this is what I want."

"The request is ridiculous," said Suhas. He crossed his arms and glared at Kunal. "Vinayak, knock some sense into this boy. He's asking us to tamper with our customers' tiffins."

A murmur rose around him, steadily growing louder as it circled the room.

"This is the only thing I want," said Kunal. "I have a job already. All I want is my family."

"Kunal, be reasonable," said Hari. "You have no idea what you're asking of us. It's too much. We want to reward your bravery but this is ... it's ..."

They all spoke at once, drowning out Hari's words.

"You weren't there!" someone said. "You didn't see how he jumped onto the tracks and not only helped Nikhil to safety, but also retrieved the last tiffin. If it hadn't been for him, we would have had at least eight customer complaints by now, not to mention all the damaged tiffins. We'd have to replace those."

"If the train had hit the carrier lying across the tracks, we would have had to contend with the Railway Authorities too," said Vinayak quietly. "Kunal has saved us a lot of trouble and expense. And yet, I'm not sure if this is the right way to repay him."

Kunal stared at Vinayak, unable to believe he'd just said that, knowing how important it was to him. His chest ached,

119

as if someone had punched him hard.

"Let him send the notes," someone said. "I don't think it's such a big deal. In fact some of our customers might even think it a great kindness, helping someone locate their family."

Agreement and dissent echoed through the room and it took the seniors a full five minutes to quiet everyone down.

"Let's take a vote," said Hari. His eyes swept the room. "Before you decide, be aware that many more customers will object to their property being misused, compared to those who would have complained about losing their tiffins."

Dubey raised his hand. Kunal's stomach dropped when Hari nodded.

"My esteemed colleagues," said Dubey. "Don't you see how wrong this is? Today it's a note, tomorrow something else. Where will it end? If you want to reward this orphan, give him clothes, some money. But please don't suggest that we play with our livelihood."

"I don't want your money," said Kunal. "I want my family." He looked around the room at the serious faces. His future was in their hands. If they said no and voted with Dubey, he'd never have this chance again. "Please, all I'm asking is for permission to send out a few notes on one day. One day. I know she's here, she's close. If there's no reply, I won't ask again."

No one uttered a word. The silence was more ominous than the buzz earlier.

Kunal was utterly exhausted. All his strength seemed to have evaporated in the muggy heat of the room. "I've got your answer," he said, looking around at the faces staring at him. "I think I'll go."

"Give us a moment," said Hari. He led his colleagues to a corner and they had a hurried discussion in whispers.

Vinayak was staring out the window and Kunal joined him.

"I know you think this is a bad idea," said Kunal. He couldn't keep the bitterness or disappointment out of his voice.

"Yes," said Vinayak, not looking at him. "You still have time to retract it. Ask for something else or become a *dabbawalla*. That's a much better future for you."

"No," said Kunal. He gripped the windowsill tightly. "My future is with my family. It's the only thing I want now."

Slowly, Vinayak faced Kunal and put his hands on his shoulders. "Be careful what you wish for, Kunal. Sometimes you might get it, only to realize it was not at all what you wanted."

"All those in favour of letting Kunal send out the notes, raise your hand," said Hari.

Kunal glanced around the room, blood roaring in his ears. Hands started rising. One third of the room. Half the room. Three-quarters of the room. Almost everyone had raised their hands except Dubey and his team members. Vinayak still had his hands behind his back.

"What about you?" Dubey asked Hari.

Hari looked steadily at him for a moment and then at Kunal. With infuriating slowness he raised his hand. A jubilant cry went around the room and Hari smiled. Kunal beamed back.

Chapter Fourteen

Vinayak was quiet on the way home and Kunal did not try and draw him out. He wanted to tell his news to every passerby, yell it out to the overcast sky and clusters of buildings huddled around him. He had to be content with humming the tune of a Hindi song he'd heard on the radio.

At the stationery store that evening, Kunal spent every rupee he had on notebooks, pencils, and erasers. Back at the *chawl*, he riffled through the pages, revelling in their newness, their inky fragrance. He caressed the lined pages; one of these would surely reach his mother. She might place her hand on the page he was touching now. They'd meet, she would beg for his forgiveness and she'd ask him to come back with her. They would be a happy family. He'd start going to school and learning interesting things, and he'd have a proper job for once.

The rest of his life neatly mapped out, he fell asleep.

Kunal awoke to the sound of a pigeon cooing. He sat up from his makeshift bed on the floor and bounded to the window. A clear blue sky stretched before him. The tattered remains of the kite in the tree had all but disappeared in yesterday's deluge, except for a very small red scrap that fluttered in the light breeze. His plan was going to work — he knew it.

The cot behind him creaked. Kunal turned around. Vinayak was already halfway to the bathroom, evidently still annoyed with him. Kunal felt the urge to run up to the old man and tell him to be happy, because he was — deliriously so. But even before he could take a step, the door shut with a soft click. Kunal turned back to the window. The red scrap waved cheerily. He smiled. Nothing could spoil his mood today.

"So, have you decided what you're going to say in the note?" asked Vinayak, as he stepped out of the bathroom, almost ready to go to work. He sounded his usual calm self and Kunal was relieved. "I'm assuming you'll want to stay back and write them."

"Yes. I have to start work with Rustom this afternoon, so I'd better work this morning."

Vinayak nodded. "I'll be back at lunchtime to help you."

"Thank you."

Kunal watched Vinayak cross the courtyard. The moment he stepped onto the sidewalk, the swiftly moving crowd engulfed him and bore him away.

What could he write that would make his mother come back? Should he plead? Be harsh? Guilt her into coming to see him? Thank God Vinayak had taught him to read and write. All those hours of hard work would come in handy now, even though he was the very person against this idea.

Kunal sat down with a clean piece of lined paper and a sharpened pencil.

"Dear Miss Patel," he wrote. Paused. No, it was too formal. He was writing to his mother, not a school teacher. He erased it.

"Dear Mother," he wrote. Stopped. No, too familiar. She might not like it. He started to erase the words. Stopped. What if he was erasing her right out of his life? He ran his finger over the words, now barely visible on the lined page. Would he ever get a chance to speak them out loud?

Kunal stared at the blank page, snatched up the pencil again and started writing.

"Dear Anahita," he wrote. Yes. This sounded right. Casual, not too friendly or distant. Now what? *This is your son, please come and get me*? This was so much harder than he had imagined.

He wandered over to the window. The crowd at the communal tap had swelled. The little boy he had seen on his first morning at the *chawl* was running around again, his mother in hot pursuit with a mug of water. Their laughter wafted up to him, along with the fragrance of freshly boiled rice. The shrill whistle of a pressure cooker pierced the muted buzz of radio commentary and conversation around him. He hadn't written one note and the inhabitants of the *chawl* were already preparing for lunch.

He strode back to the desk and started writing, not pausing to think, letting his heart seep onto the page through his fingertips.

Dear Anahita,

*You left something with Mrs. Seth twelve years
ago. Why didn't you come back for it? What
happened? I must know. If nothing else, you owe
me an explanation.*

Kunal
PS: I'm not at the dhaba *anymore. I'm with
Vinayak at the* dabbawalla chawl *at 51, Janpath
Lane in Andheri, third floor, room five. I'm the
boy with the green eyes.*

Kunal stared at the note. His deepest desire stared back at
him. He folded the page. Waited a whole minute. Then he
unfolded it and tried to read it once again, trying to imagine
his mother reading it. He had deliberately not given too
much detail so that a stranger reading it would not know
what it was about. No one would understand the note
except his mother. And green eyes were so rare in Bombay,
she was sure to recognize him when they met.

But would she respond? Or would she crumple his plea
into a ball and throw it away? There was only one way to
find out and that was to send out as many as possible, and
hope.

He had the sudden urge to read the note his mother had
written all those years ago. He pulled it out from under
the mattress and laid it alongside his own, comparing her
neat handwriting with his large, ill-formed letters. All those

years ago she too had written a note, put it in a tiffin, and sent it to his father. Now, twelve years later, he was doing the same. But her note hadn't reached his father. Was his note doomed to failure too?

A cold hand clutched at his heart and he held his head in his hands trying to rid himself of the feeling of utter futility. This time it had to work. His mother had sent one note. He was going to send many, as many as he could write.

Should he wait to show this note to Vinayak? He decided not to, not when time was so short and he had but one chance to send them out. Kunal pulled the notebooks apart and started copying out the wording. Five, ten, fifteen notes piled up beside him. After a while the words were emblazoned across his mind's eye so that he did not need to copy them. His hand moved automatically across the blank page.

The door opened and Kunal looked up with a start. Vinayak stepped into the room with a parcel that gave off the most delectable fragrance. "Lunchtime," he said.

Kunal stood up, massaging his cramped fingers. "Oh good! I'm so hungry I could eat an elephant."

"Sorry, you'll have to make do with a goat!" said Vinayak, holding aloft a parcel of food.

Kunal stared at him blankly till he noticed the twinkle in the old man's eye. "Oh, I see," he said, smiling. If Vinayak was joking it meant he'd accepted Kunal's plan.

"How did you fare with the notes?"

"Seventeen," said Kunal with a mournful look.

"I'll help you after lunch." Kunal smiled gratefully as they sat down to a delicious lunch of mutton biryani and *raita*. After they had eaten, Vinayak put on his glasses and picked up a note. He scanned the page quickly and slumped in his chair.

"What do you think?" asked Kunal. "Will she come?"

Vinayak sighed deeply. "Kunal, this is a good letter, cleverly written, too. But you realize that this may not work, don't you? Someone who left you all those years ago is not going to come back just because you wrote a touching note, no matter how badly you want them to."

Kunal felt the familiar tug of anger and sadness in his chest. Why did Vinayak always have to dampen his spirits? He finally had a chance to find his mother and all he was getting from Vinayak was endless caution and gloom. What was wrong with this old man?

"You belong somewhere, the *dabbawalla* community," said Kunal, trying not to snap. "Is it so wrong for me to want to belong somewhere too?"

"If there was any hope in it, I would have encouraged you, Kunal. But this is next to useless and I wish you would trust me when I tell you this is a really bad idea, and a waste of time and money."

Trust. That treacherous word again. He thought of Mrs. Seth and all the lies she'd told him, and though he knew now they were for his own good, he'd trusted her and been betrayed. Had he known about the letter, he would have started the search for his mother much sooner. He remembered the conversation with his trusted friend, Lalan, in the stinking dishwashing room when he told Kunal he was leaving for good. He wanted to trust Vinayak but it was hard, so very hard.

"I have to do this," said Kunal. "If you can't encourage me, then please don't say anything at all."

Vinayak looked at him for a long moment. "All right, Kunal. I can see you're determined to see this through," he said. "I promised to help and so I shall." Without another word he pulled the pile of blank pages towards him and started copying out the note.

All too soon it was time for Kunal to report to work at Sunshine. He almost wished he had waited a few days before accepting the job but he had spent the last of his money on the notebooks. He needed more, and fast, so that he could contribute to the meals and other expenses, even though he knew Vinayak didn't expect it.

"I'll be back after midnight," said Kunal.

Vinayak nodded. "Be careful when you're returning at night. Keep to the main roads."

"Of course," said Kunal.

Lalan's battered face still haunted his dreams.

The climb to the third floor of the *chawl* seemed like he was scaling Mount Everest. Panting hard and tired to his very core, Kunal stepped into the corridor. Light spilled from room number five where a crowd milled around near the entrance. A mound of *chappals* littered the doorway and the *dabbawallas* were probing it with their feet, trying to find their respective pairs. Kunal's heart galloped and his tiredness vanished. Why the crowd? Had something happened to Vinayak?

He raced along the narrow corridor. "What happened?

128

Why are all of you here?"

"Kunal's back," one of the *dabbawallas* sang out. "Our very own Amitabh Bachchan is here." More people trickled out of the room, laughing and joking.

"Are you having a party without me?" said Kunal. He tried to peek into the room but there were too many people in the corridor, blocking the doorway.

"Yes," said Nikhil, who'd just walked out. "But it's over now. Good night." He had a huge grin on his face.

"Oh," said Kunal, glad his face was in the shadows.

"Bye, see you tomorrow," said Moray.

"Good night," another called out.

"Good morning!" someone else corrected.

Kunal flattened himself against the wall as the men filed past, smiling. His guts twisted. They'd obviously had a great time while he was away. He did not belong to their family and they hadn't included him in their celebrations. The sense of belonging to no one crushed him. He took a deep breath. With any luck he'd have someone of his own, soon. He wouldn't be lonely ever again.

Finally, Kunal was able to enter the room. He stopped in the doorway, aghast. Instead of the remains of a party, piles of paper covered every surface, even the floor. Vinayak sat on the cot massaging his hand. He saw Kunal and managed a smile that looked more like a grimace.

"How was the first day?"

"What's this?" squeaked Kunal.

"Notes," said Vinayak. "They all wanted to help."

"But I thought most of them hadn't learned to write,"

said Kunal.

"Yes, but they can copy out letters," said Vinayak.

For a moment, Kunal could only stare into Vinayak's red-rimmed eyes. Then he whirled around and ran back outside. The *dabbawallas* were still in sight; black shadows gliding across the courtyard and scattering as they went — some heading to other sections of the *chawl* and some towards the main street.

"THANK YOU!" yelled Kunal, waving frantically. "Thanks a lot!"

"You're welcome," a chorus of voices replied. "Any time!"

Lights came on in some of the darkened rooms of the *chawl*. A few choice curses flew at him.

"Oi, it's one a.m. Go to sleep or I'll come up there and put you to sleep."

"Shut up, stupid!"

Kunal hurried back inside, unable to stop smiling. His tiredness had vanished completely. He looked at the notes again, flitting from one pile to another, running his finger along its height.

"This is ... this is unbelievable," he said. "There must be hundreds here!"

"Yes," said Vinayak.

"Thank you," said Kunal. His voice trembled. "They must have helped because they think the world of you."

Vinayak gave a tired smile. "Not just me. You have a few loyal followers too."

Kunal picked up one of the notes. The handwriting was shaky but legible. There was also a PPS that read,

*If you know an Anahita Patel in finance, please
pass this note to her.*

"This is brilliant," said Kunal. "This little bit at the end.
There can't be too many Anahita Patels who are financial
analysts downtown."

"Yes," said Vinayak. "That was Nikhil's idea. We added
that line to all the notes you'd written too."

Kunal lay down, too excited to sleep. Tomorrow hundreds
of these notes would be on their way to find his mother. And
one would reach her. How could it not? His face turned warm
when he remembered that he'd cursed the *dabbawallas* for
not including him in their party when all along, he'd been
the virtual guest of honour.

He made a promise to himself; no matter where he was,
how rich and successful he became, he would never forget
the *dabbawallas*, or their kindness.

"Wake up, Kunal," said Vinayak. "We'd better get to the
station extra early today."

Kunal opened his eyes and sat up. A brilliant slab of
sunshine lay by the window, neatly sliced into bars. "What
time is it?"

"Seven."

Kunal jumped to his feet and made another circuit of the
room, touching the notes. Yesterday hadn't been a dream.
"I still can't believe it," he said.

"You'll believe it when you're lugging them all the way
to the station," said Vinayak. "Let's get going."

"How many are there?" said Kunal

"I lost count after three hundred," said Vinayak. "But it's just a little over that figure."

"But ... but I didn't buy enough notebooks," said Kunal. Even as he said that, he knew. Vinayak had paid for the extra books. "How will I ever repay you?"

"I'll think of something," said Vinayak. "You can be sure of that."

When Kunal hurried out of the bathroom, ready to face the day, the notes were already by the door in six large plastic bags.

"We should be able to manage these," said Vinayak, picking up three bags effortlessly. "Right?"

Kunal scooped up the other three, feeling his shoulders sag with the strain, and followed Vinayak. The streets looked clean and even the beggars seemed less pathetic on this bright and sunny morning. He smiled at everyone he passed and got glares in return. He didn't care.

At the station they waited at their usual spot. As each *dabbawalla* walked in, Vinayak counted the number of tiffins in his carrier and handed him the exact number of notes with instructions to put them on top of the tiffins, inside the aluminum cases, before sorting them. This way, the notes would be the first thing the customers would see when they opened their lunch boxes that afternoon.

The excitement was palpable as everyone took part in Kunal's project with gusto — everyone except sour-faced Dubey and his team, who huddled and whispered among themselves. Dubey glanced over a couple of times and shook his head. He'd announced just moments before that his team would not distribute the notes and if any of the tiffins he was delivering had them, he'd throw them out.

"What if my mother happens to be working in the building that Dubey's team is delivering to?" said Kunal. "She won't get the notes because his team won't take them."

"Stop it, Kunal. It will do you no good thinking of the 'ifs' and 'buts,'" said Vinayak. "Anyway, most of the financial district deliveries are made by my people and many others who want to help. So stop worrying and start distributing."

Kunal flitted nervously from one carrier to another, opening the aluminum cases to check his note was right on top.

"You'd better stop doing that," said Moray. "The food will get cold. Then we'll really have upset customers."

"Sorry," said Kunal. Heat crept up his neck. He was getting carried away, and the last thing he wanted was for the customers to complain about cold food.

"We'll find her, don't you worry!" said Moray. "She can't escape us ... the *dabbawallas* are everywhere and Bombay is our backyard!"

Kunal looked at Moray, a lump in his throat. How willingly he and the others had jumped in to help him. These were friends to whom he'd be indebted for life, whether the plan succeeded or not.

A crackly voice announced the arrival of the ten a.m. train to Churchgate and the *dabbawallas* hoisted the carriers onto their heads, readying themselves for the usual mad dash.

Kunal stood aside and riffled through the remaining

notes trying to stay still. He couldn't. He paced, glancing at the clock, the crowds, and the carriers, wishing he could fast-forward the hour to three in the afternoon when the *dabbawallas* would be returning, hopefully one of them bearing good news. The wait hadn't even begun and already it was unbearable.

Nikhil came up to Kunal. "Let me have those extra notes. I'll pass them on to some of my friends at the interconnecting stations. We'll find her," he said with a wink.

Kunal gave him a bear hug. After Lalan, he had been so afraid to let anyone get close, but Nikhil had been irresistible. Nikhil's friendship was worth daring to trust again. Kunal was going to miss him the most when he left. "Thanks," he said, and he gave the notes to Nikhil.

"Mention not!" Nikhil tucked the notes into the front of his shirt, hoisted the carrier on his head and hurried off towards the platform.

The train chugged into the station. The *dabbawallas* boarded several compartments, then waved to him as the train slid out of the station and picked up speed. Vinayak stood beside him, his arm around Kunal's shoulder.

Kunal stared at the receding tail lights of the train. It had begun. In less than two hours a large number of Bombayites would be reading his note, and he prayed one of them would be his mother.

There was something terribly wrong with the clock at Sunshine. It was running so slow that Kunal wondered if the batteries were dying. Once the lunchtime rush died down, he would tell Rustom about it, maybe go and buy new batteries.

Noon. A customer beckoned to him and ordered something. Kunal could only think of the notes; all the tiffins would have been delivered by now.

"Hey, you idiot!" yelled the customer he had just served.

Kunal snapped out of his reverie. "What?"

"I'd ordered mutton cutlets, not an omelette."

One p.m. Kunal dropped a cup of scalding tea steps away from the pickup counter. He had tripped while staring at a woman and trying to imagine what his mother would look like. Just a few drops landed on a customer sitting close by who nevertheless howled in protest. He shut up after Rustom offered him a cream cake on the house.

Two p.m. Kunal stood mesmerized by the hands of the clock. They didn't seem to be moving at all. He was sure the batteries had died. Someone smacked the back of his head. Kunal jumped almost a foot off the ground, thinking Sethji had found him.

"*Saala gadhera*," said Rustom. "You've done nothing but stare at the clock all morning and mess up all your orders. You want to be fired?"

"I-I ...," said Kunal. He stopped. How could he explain what was going on without sounding like a complete fool?

"You've never been this inattentive. What's the matter?"

Kunal decided to be completely honest. "I have to get to the station. The *dabbawallas* are helping me look for my mother today and they may have news."

Rustom blew air out of his cheeks as he stared at Kunal.

135

Then he sat down at the nearest vacant table. "Sit," he said to Kunal.

Kunal obeyed, his eyes instinctively going to the clock again. 2:01.

"Does Vinayak know?" said Rustom.

"He's the one who helped me the most," said Kunal. "Can I take the rest of the afternoon off and go to the station? I promise to make up the time tomorrow."

"On one condition," said Rustom. He was studying Kunal's face as if it were the *Midday* newspaper.

"Anything," said Kunal. He stole another glance at the clock. 2:03.

"No matter what happens, I want you back at work tomorrow," said Rustom. "All right?"

Kunal nodded. He'd agree to anything right now. He just wanted to get out.

"Then go!"

Kunal jumped to his feet and ran off before Rustom could change his mind. Only when he was halfway to the station, panting hard as he waited for the lights to change, did he realize what Rustom had really meant. If he wanted Kunal to report to work the next day, Rustom was already certain he wouldn't find his mother.

Kunal stood still, waiting for the walk sign. And when it did come on, he couldn't walk. He slumped against the telephone pole, staring at the busy road. Rustom was wrong. So was Vinayak. He would find her and she would take him to live with her.

Kunal raced into the station. His eyes shot to the clock as

he skidded to a halt. Two-thirty. He still had half an hour before the *dabbawallas* would start coming back. There was a lone *dabbawalla* sitting on a bench facing the tracks. Kunal did not need to see his face to figure out who it was. He sat down beside Vinayak and waited.

Two forty-five. Kunal's stomach churned as the first train ground to a halt, bringing with it a whiff of day-old fish. The crowd parted easily to let a dozen fisherwomen through, with their baskets perched atop their heads and dripping foul-smelling water. Right behind them followed the first *dabbawalla*. Kunal ran up to him. The man shook his head before heading to the regular spot to await the others. The tiffins would be sorted in reverse now and returned to the owners. Kunal shuffled back to the bench.

"This is just the first one," said Vinayak. "Don't be disheartened."

Kunal took a deep breath. Two more trains went by. There were no *dabbawallas* in either. His heart spiralled down to his toes. He wanted to throw up, but reminded himself he'd had no lunch. A terrible fear gnawed at his stomach.

A *dabbawalla* whose route included the Air India building and the Bombay Stock Exchange got off the next train and hurried towards them with a grim expression. Right away Kunal knew: bad news.

"What is it?" asked Kunal even before the man could speak.

"Nothing on the notes, Kunal, but you and Vinayak have to go to the office right away. Moray told me just as I was boarding the train at Bandra."

"Why?" asked Vinayak.

"Some customers have already telephoned the Association to complain about the notes. They claim this is advertising they're paying for," continued the man, "and they're demanding a discount on their monthly fees."

Fear ballooned inside him. He could barely breathe. Hari had warned them about this. And now it had really happened. Could people be so petty about a note?

Vinayak nodded. "We'll go right away."

"No!" said Kunal. "I want to wait till all the *dabbawallas* get in. You go without me."

"Stop it," said Vinayak. His voice was ice-cold despite the muggy heat that enveloped them. "When Hari calls, we have to go. If anyone has news, they'll know where to find us."

Instead of walking, they took a train to the head office. Kunal was quiet. A part of him knew Vinayak was right, and yet, he hated having to leave the station. What if one of them had found her? And what if she had accompanied the *dabbawalla* back to Andheri Station? He shook his head, trying to clear away the possibilities and questions that plagued him.

"Is this really very bad?" asked Kunal as they neared the building. "What will they do to me? It was my idea, after all."

"Don't worry about it, Kunal. Hari did give you his permission; he even voted for you, remember?"

The climb up to the first floor seemed shorter than before, as if someone had magically whisked away a few stairs. All too soon they were stepping into the office. Hari looked up from the discussion he had been having with Suhas and

138

Param. A few *dabbawallas* stood in groups, chatting. All eyes swivelled towards them. The silence in the room was thicker and heavier than the air before a thunderstorm.

"Customer complaints are pouring in by the minute," said Hari without preamble. "How many notes were sent out?"

"A little over three hundred," replied Vinayak after a moment's thought.

"Three hundred?" whispered Hari. He shook his head sorrowfully. "You mean we might get three hundred complaints? How could you write so many notes in such a short time?"

Kunal didn't say a word.

"I don't believe everyone is going to complain," said Vinayak. "Who knows, some might even be sympathetic to Kunal's cause."

"I wish I hadn't allowed it," said Hari. He stared at Kunal. "I don't know what's going to happen. Those that have complained are demanding a discount. If word spreads, our entire customer base might want one. We just can't afford something like this. We're already charging rock-bottom prices."

"But why?" asked Kunal. "They put notes into their tiffins too. What we did is no different."

Hari frowned. "Let me put it this way: suppose you wrote a letter, sealed the envelope, put a stamp on, and mailed it. During its journey to the post office, the postman opened up your letter and stuck in a letter of his own and then mailed it. Would you be all right with that?"

Kunal shook his head.

"That's exactly what we've done. You're using the customer's envelope to mail your own letter. Without their permission."

The crowd in the room had been steadily swelling.

Dubey marched in, furious and red-faced. He wagged a finger at Hari. "I told you all not to do it! I warned you this would happen and yet you allowed it. Now see the mess we're in?"

"You keep that finger of yours down," snapped Hari. "I am still the senior-most member of this Association. No one points a finger at me."

Glowering, Dubey lowered his hand. The seniors held a hurried discussion. After a few moments, Hari faced them again. There was immediate silence.

"The only way to appease the affected customers is to give them a twenty-five rupee discount on their delivery fee for next month. This way we won't lose anyone."

An angry hiss circulated the room.

"We're already earning so little, how can we take a pay cut?"

"No way! We can't afford it."

"We'll issue a public apology. They can take it or leave it."

Kunal looked around at the motley faces; some old, some thin, many looking exhausted and haggard. These men worked very hard, carrying loads up to forty kilograms back and forth each day, for a meagre sum. He'd never looked beyond their uniforms but now, he took a good long look. These were poor men with large families to feed and because of his selfish request they might go hungry next month. A wave of shame washed over him; he had snatched food from their mouths.

"I'm so very sorry —," he started to say, but Hari cut in.

"What's done is done, Kunal. You did not force us, we did it of our own free will and now we have to face the consequences. We shall all be a bit leaner and wiser next month. Param, issue an announcement to our customers about the discount."

"Troublemaker!" spat Dubey. He stomped off with his sycophants.

Some of the *dabbawallas* drifted away, not meeting Kunal's eyes. Those who did gave him a small nod and walked away. A few came up to him and patted him on the back.

"Any luck with the notes?" he asked those who approached him. All he got was a shake of the head and a "Sorry."

Within minutes the room was empty.

"Shall we go?" said Vinayak quietly.

Kunal shuffled to the door, then stopped and whirled round. He couldn't stop the tears spilling out. "Aren't you going to tell me 'I told you so'?"

"No," said Vinayak quietly. He put an arm around Kunal. "Let's go home."

Chapter Fifteen

"*Arre saala gadhera*," Rustom called out. "Why such a long face? You'll put me out of business, boy! And stop scrubbing that table; you've already taken six inches off the Formica."

Kunal looked up from the table he had been wiping over and over for the last five minutes. "Sorry," he said and tried to look cheerful.

"Oh please," said Rustom, spreading his hands in mock horror. "If that horrible thing you just did was meant to be a smile, I'd rather you didn't."

"Sorry," Kunal repeated. "You want me to help out in the kitchen?"

"You stay right here where I can keep an eye on you," said Rustom. "You'll curdle the milk with one look, *gadhera*!"

"All right," said Kunal. "But why do you keep calling me that? What are you really saying?"

"Why do you want to know?"

Kunal shrugged. "Just asking," he said, "but if you'd rather go on abusing me using words I don't know ..."

"Okay, you can stop with the melodrama," Rustom cut in. "It means donkey."

"What — you've been calling me a donkey all this while? Why?"

"What's wrong with it?" said Rustom. "They're hardworking and trustworthy animals."

Kunal shook his head and walked away, aware that Rustom had paid him a backhanded compliment. He knew the proprietor was trying to cheer him up, but he was not in the mood to be happy. Late-afternoon sunshine poured into Sunshine, but it couldn't reach his black thoughts. It had been three days since the notes had gone out. She *still* hadn't contacted him. What had he expected? That his mother would take the next train to Andheri Station and sweep him into her arms?

He scrunched up the rag in his fist. Yes, that was exactly what he had hoped for, prayed for.

After Sethji's taunts and brutal beatings he thought he could bear any kind of pain. How wrong he was.

A customer wandered into the shop and sat down. Kunal went up to him immediately, glad for something to do. The man ordered tea and a cream cake. Kunal waited at the kitchen counter, his thoughts drifting once more. Vinayak had been right. His mother had abandoned him deliberately. Mrs. Seth had also been right when she'd said that he would never find her.

Why hadn't he listened to them? How the *dabbawallas* must hate him at this moment.

The kitchen helper put a wedge of cake on the pickup counter, its surface covered with frozen waves of pink cream and, alongside it, a steaming glass of tea. Kunal took them over to the customer, wrote the bill on a small chit of paper, and put it on the table.

"I'll have a tea, please," said a familiar voice.

Kunal whipped around. There was Vinayak by the window, a newspaper spread out on the table. A sense of déjà vu swept over him. How often had he seen Vinayak exactly this way while he worked at the *dhaba*. This old man had been the one bright spot in his day. Now, Vinayak must hate him for embarrassing him in front of the *dabbawalla* community.

"Just tea?" asked Kunal. "Something to eat? Maybe a mutton pattie? They're fresh."

Vinayak shook his head. "Just tea, thanks." His expression was calm, and yet his eyes shone as if he was trying hard to keep a secret from spilling out.

"Right away," said Kunal, and he hurried to the counter.

"Where's my bill?" asked Vinayak when Kunal brought his tea a few moments later.

"This one's on me," said Kunal.

"Thank you. Can you sit for a moment?"

Kunal looked around. The restaurant was almost empty except for the one customer who had ordered the cake and tea. He was digging into it with gusto, pink cream flecking his thick black moustache. Kunal perched on the edge of a chair.

"I know you're upset — about the notes, and with me," said Vinayak.

"Why should I be?" said Kunal. He avoided looking into those eyes, which could see straight into his heart. He stared at the scratched countertop instead. Some of the cuts ran so deep, repairing them would be impossible. Rustom would have to replace the entire tabletop. If only *he* could do the same: throw away his old life — scratches, scars, and all. Get a brand new one — a happy one.

"I know you wanted to find your family," said Vinayak. "I understand that because I want mine back too, so badly I can taste it. But wanting does not guarantee getting."

Kunal stared out the window.

"You think you have it rough, Kunal? Feeling sorry for yourself? Snap out of it! You have your health, a job, and me. Things could be worse. Far, far worse." Vinayak's voice had dropped to a whisper.

"You never told me what happened. Who did you lose?" said Kunal. He was quite sure Vinayak would avoid telling him yet again.

"My wife *and* my son," said Vinayak quietly. "He was only ten when he died."

Kunal gripped the edge of the table, staring at that deeply lined face. His wife and son! How unbearable that must be. "How ... when ...," he asked, his voice cracking as the enormity of the news sunk in.

"Twelve years ago," said Vinayak. He ran his finger around the rim of the glass of tea. Around and around and around. "They were taking a rickshaw to the head office where we were supposed to meet." Vinayak looked up, his face pale. "You see, I hated it when they were late. I'd get very annoyed with them. Punctuality was ingrained in me; it was my life's mission as a *dabbawalla*. And so, to avoid my anger, my wife decided to take a rickshaw."

Around and around went Vinayak's finger. The glass
squeaked. Car horns blared outside. Kunal sat quietly waiting
for Vinayak to continue. What a heavy burden he'd been
carrying all by himself for the last twelve years.

"Then?" said Kunal.

"The rickshaw collided head-on with a truck. No one
survived." He said it in a matter-of-fact voice. His finger
trembled as it traversed the rim of the glass. A drop of water
fell into the tea, setting up ripples on its surface. Vinayak
pushed the glass away and looked out the window, wiping
his eyes with his sleeve.

"I'm so sorry," said Kunal. And he was. Both their lives
had changed, irrevocably, twelve years ago. He had lost his
family without knowing it, but how much worse it must
have been for Vinayak to have loved and then lost them. He
just couldn't find the words to take away the pain that filled
the old man's eyes. How badly he must want them back,
but that didn't mean he'd get them back. Ever. And that is
what Vinayak had been trying to tell him about his mother.

"I'm sorry too," said Vinayak after a long moment. "Sorry
that you'll never see your family. But there is something I
want to ask you. I've been thinking about it for a few days.
You don't have to give me an answer right away. Just think
about it, okay?"

Kunal squeezed Vinayak's hand. "Whatever it is,
Vinayakji," he said, "you have only to ask."

"I'd like you to stay with me. For good."

"What?"

"You heard me."

This was so unexpected that it was Kunal's turn to look away as his mind groped for words that just wouldn't come to him. It was like trying to catch smoke. Vinayak had said this was a temporary arrangement. Now, Kunal had a chance at a permanent home and a father.

Kunal looked at Vinayak. He'd never seen him that way. And what about his real mother? Should he abandon the idea to look for her, just as she had abandoned him?

"If you think about it, we're both in search of the same thing, aren't we?" said Vinayak. "When I saw you four years ago at the *dhaba*, you reminded me of my lost son. You're so like him. Kunal, are you all right? I'm sorry if I've upset you ..."

Kunal shook his head, blushing deeply. "No, no, I'm not upset. It's just that ... you see, I wasn't expecting ... but thank you. I-I'm so ..."

"KUNAL!"

Rustom's paper flew into the air and both Vinayak and Kunal shot to their feet.

Nikhil burst into the restaurant out of breath. His eyes sparkled and he couldn't stop grinning.

"Oi, *junglee*!" yelled Rustom. "Did you have to make such a dramatic entrance? You almost gave me a heart attack," he said.

Nikhil ignored him and ran up to Kunal. "We've ...," he gasped, "we've found her! At least, we think we have."

"Found whom?" asked Kunal, his pulse racing, though he knew Nikhil could only be referring to one person.

147

"Your mother! We found her!"

Kunal shook his head. "You're not pulling my leg, are you? Tell me this isn't some joke."

"No, no, NO!" said Nikhil. He grasped Kunal by the shoulders and shook him hard. "You remember those extra notes you gave me?"

Kunal nodded. He shot a glance at Vinayak, who was listening intently.

"I wasn't able to distribute them all, so I kept them. I decided to hand them out to a couple of *dabbawallas* in the financial district who are quite friendly with their customers. I know ... don't look at me like that, Vinayakji ... I know it was against the rules, but I so desperately wanted to help Kunal. My friends requested their customers to circulate the notes within their offices. One of them who delivers tiffins to Mittal Towers just came back with the news. He said he was waiting by the elevator on the third floor when he noticed this well-dressed woman reading something and crying as if her heart would break. He felt sorry for her and asked if he could help. He happened to glance at what she was reading. It was your note, Kunal! She was reading your note and crying!"

"See, Vinayakji?" said Kunal. "I told you I'd find her. I was right after all."

The afternoon sun illuminated the sickly pallor of Vinayak's face. He managed a small smile as he wiped the beads of sweat from his forehead. "This is such exciting news, I have to sit down," he said. He lowered himself into a chair, groaning softly.

Nikhil hadn't finished yet. He grabbed Vinayak's glass of cold tea from the table and downed it in one gulp. "Thirsty," he said, wiping his mouth with the back of his hand.

"Are you absolutely sure?" asked Kunal. He had a hard time keeping his voice steady. All of him was trembling. "This isn't some mistake, is it? Did he get her address, her number?"

Nikhil shook his head. "*Arre baba*, wait! I'm coming to it."

"Hurry up," growled Kunal.

"My friend told her he'd been the one to distribute the notes. She was shocked. She asked him if he'd seen you. Unfortunately, you've not met him — he picks up his deliveries from another station — so he had to say no."

Kunal couldn't breathe. She was asking about him. She cared. She still loved him!

"Where does she live? Did he get her number? Can I call her right now?"

Nikhil scratched his head. "That's where we have a problem."

"What problem?" said Kunal. His stomach dropped. He was sure he was not going to like the answer.

"She didn't give her number, though my friend asked her a couple of times. He said she looked a bit scared."

"I see," said Kunal. But he didn't see at all.

"But she did say she'd come to see you," said Nikhil. "Very soon!"

Kunal gripped the back of the chair, afraid his legs might give way at any moment. "Can you take me to see her?"

149

"We can go now if you like," said Nikhil. "We still have an hour before the office closes and the receptionist should be able to find her easily."

"Let's go," said Kunal.

Just then there was a loud crash. Vinayak lay on the floor, drenched in sweat, clutching his chest.

Chapter Sixteen

Kunal peered in through the glass-panelled swinging doors of the triage area. Rows of green curtains hid the sick from anxious eyes. A lone doctor and two harried nurses scurried from one enclosed area to another, looking as pale and ill as the patients that were wheeled in and out.

Another screaming ambulance drew up at the doors of the emergency room. Kunal clapped his hands to his ears. Each time he heard the siren he remembered the interminable ride from Sunshine Restaurant to the hospital beside an unconscious Vinayak. He remembered clutching Vinayak's cold hands in a tight grip, as if he could prevent the unthinkable. His eyes had darted between the ambulance staff and Vinayak, expecting to hear the dreaded words at any moment. But Vinayak had held on and was still in there somewhere, fighting for his life.

More patients arrived; some came on their own and some were wheeled in by an attendant. A victim of a car accident was pushed through on a gurney. His face was smashed and bleeding. Kunal gagged and turned away, reaching for the nearest chair. He took deep breaths and shook his head, trying to dislodge the horror, the dizziness, and the panic that had his mind firmly in their grip.

"He'll be all right," whispered Nikhil, and squeezed Kunal's shoulder. Kunal shrugged Nikhil's hand away and peeked through the glass again.

An hour ticked by, then four. A one-way tide of the sick and injured flowed past, but Kunal scarcely noticed. His eyes were glued to the swinging doors that led to the bowels of the hospital, and to Vinayak. Every time he approached the doors a stern male nurse sent him back to his seat.

"When he's ready to see someone, we'll let you know," he'd said once. After that, his glare had deterred Kunal from asking for the umpteenth time if he could go in.

Kunal perched at the edge of a chair, his head in his hands, staring at the tiled floor flecked with brown. They looked like spots of dried blood. He looked away. Had Vinayak died and no one wanted to convey the news to him? Or maybe they'd forgotten someone had accompanied the old man to the hospital and was waiting for news. They certainly had their hands full with the living ones who poured into the hospital like the monsoon floods.

Kunal imagined leaving the hospital and going back alone to the empty room in the *chawl*. Vinayak had become so much a part of his life that to think of carrying on without him made his throat ache.

Unable to sit still any longer, Kunal marched over to the registration desk. A slim nurse with extremely dark skin, dressed in a starched white *saree*, was frantically doing paperwork. She barely glanced up as Kunal approached.

"I want to see Vinayak," he said in what he hoped was a polite yet firm voice.

The phone rang. The nurse answered it. "No, don't bring any more here. The beds are full. Take them to Jaslok Hospital. They have ten beds left."

Kunal glared at her.

"Maybe we should come back later," said Nikhil. "She looks really busy."

"Shut up," said Kunal. "They can't ignore us forever. And if you don't want to be here, then go home and inform the others."

Nikhil's face coloured and Kunal felt a pang. He was taking out his anger on the wrong person. It should be this nurse or the doctor who refused to tell him what was going on.

"I'm busy," she said, not even looking at them. "Go back to your seat and we'll —"

"At least tell me if Vinayak is alive or dead!" shouted Kunal, thumping his fist on the desk. The words spilled out along with his tears, neither of which he could hold back any longer.

The nurse looked up then and her face softened. "Isn't there anyone else with you? Your parents?"

Kunal shook his head, afraid that the sobs crowding his throat would overpower his words.

"Vinayak," said the nurse consulting a file. "You're talking about the old man in the white *kurta* pyjama who was brought in four hours ago, right?"

"Yes," said Nikhil.

She picked up the phone, dialled a number, and murmured into the mouthpiece. The siren of another approaching ambulance drowned out her whisper. She replaced the receiver and looked at them, her eyes serious.

"How are you related to the patient? Only family is allowed to see him."

Kunal took a deep breath. "I'm his son, his only family," he said. He had never been so sure of anything.

"Oh."

"So can I see him?"

The nurse stood up and came round the desk. She beckoned and led them to the swinging doors where the male attendant stood guard. Kunal gripped Nikhil's arm tightly as they followed her.

"Vinayak's son," said Nikhil with a slight smile. "We'll get to see him now."

Kunal did not reply.

"Take them to the ICU. Patient's name is Vinayak Gogte. Heart attack," said the nurse.

"Thank you," said Kunal. "Thank you so much. But he's all right, isn't he? He'll live?"

"You will have to ask the doctor about that," she said.

"Why can't you tell us?" demanded Kunal. "You spoke to someone inside — you must know."

The nurse's expression hardened. "Because I'm not allowed to."

"He's just worried," Nikhil piped in. "Sorry. And thank you, Miss."

The nurse nodded and walked back to her desk. They

followed the attendant deeper and deeper into the hospital, the chaos of the emergency room fading away with each step. The smell of antiseptic grew stronger and the only sounds now were the buzz and hum of machinery. After walking through a labyrinth of bleached corridors bathed in stark white light, they reached another set of doors with the letters ICU painted in bold black.

"What does that mean?" asked Nikhil, hanging back a little.

"Intensive Care Unit," replied the attendant. "It's where the very ill patients stay until they're better."

Kunal's heart slammed against his ribs. "So now what?" he said. "Can we go in and look for him?"

Before the attendant could reply, the doors swung open and a tall man in a white coat stepped out.

"These two are here to see Vinayak Gogte," said the attendant.

The doctor consulted the clipboard he was carrying. "Are either of you related to him?" he asked.

"I'm his son," said Kunal. The words rolled off his lips smoothly this time and he felt no hesitation — just a deep sense of how right the word *son* felt.

"He's had a severe heart attack, but he's stable now. We've done all we can to make him comfortable," said the doctor. "But we'll need to watch him for a couple of days. Go home and rest. You can see him tomorrow."

"Can I see him now?" said Kunal. "I've been waiting for hours. Please, Doctor?"

The doctor hesitated.

"Just one look so I know he's all right, and then I'll go. I promise."

The doctor nodded. "All right, but only one of you can go in. Just for a couple of minutes." He ducked his head inside the door and called out softly for a nurse.

Kunal could only bob his head in thanks, afraid that if he opened his mouth he'd embarrass himself and disturb every occupant of the ICU. The doctor patted his shoulder and strode away.

"I'll wait here," said Nikhil, and once again Kunal nodded.

He followed the nurse through the swinging doors. As he passed each curtained area he heard the whoosh and hiss of machines, a rattle of breath, the creak of a bed. The nurse stopped before a cubicle at the very end of the room. She grasped the curtain and looked at him.

"Don't be scared by what you see; it's normal," she said. Her words made his pulse race. What was he about to see? She drew back the curtain. It folded on itself with a whirring sound that seemed too loud in the surrounding buzz.

Kunal stared at his friend lying in the hospital bed and shuddered. There was so much more bed than Vinayak. Tubes and wires were attached to his chest and arms, and a huge machine behind him hummed and beeped. It seemed like it was sucking the life out of him rather than keeping him alive.

"I'm going to check on another patient. I'll be back in a couple of minutes," the nurse whispered. "Don't touch anything. If he wakes, don't let him talk; he's very weak."

Kunal barely heard her. All he could think of was the

156

last conversation they had had, the look in Vinayak's eyes when he had asked Kunal to stay with him for good. He approached the bed cautiously. There was a medicinal smell in the room that made him uneasy. It was freezing. Kunal's heart thudded so loudly, he hoped it wouldn't wake Vinayak.

He sat at the edge of the bed. Vinayak's eyes fluttered and Kunal jerked to his feet, staring at him. The machine hissed and a green dot bounced across a screen on the wall above Vinayak's bed. It was the only thing in here that seemed happy. Vinayak's eyes remained closed.

Kunal was overcome by his need to touch the old man, to feel his warm skin under his fingertips. Kunal reached out and traced the veins in Vinayak's hand, which stood out in sharp relief. A needle stuck out of one, held in place by white gauze taped to it. This must really hurt, he thought. He heard a soft groan and looked up. Vinayak was awake and watching him.

The crushing weight on Kunal's chest lightened. He took a deep breath. "How are you?"

"Okay," whispered Vinayak. He swallowed, his Adam's apple bobbing under the wrinkled skin of his throat. He looked so fragile. "Kunal, I ..."

"Shhhh." Kunal put a finger on Vinayak's lips. Their warmth was so reassuring that Kunal almost lost his composure. He peered round the curtain. "Please, don't say any more. The nurse will get angry with me. You're supposed to rest."

"Go ..." Vinayak whispered. "Mother."

Kunal looked deep into Vinayak's eyes. What he saw

157

terrified him. They were the eyes of a person who had decided to give up. On him. On everything.

He moved closer to Vinayak and knelt by the bed, willing the old man to look into his eyes, his heart, like he used to. "I'm not going anywhere," said Kunal. "You said you wanted me to stay with you for good. I'm holding you to that promise."

Vinayak closed his eyes and his breathing deepened, but not before Kunal noticed that the spark had returned. The fight was back on.

He stood up as soon as he heard footsteps approaching. The nurse drew the curtains around Vinayak and then walked Kunal out of the ICU quietly.

"How is he doing?" asked Nikhil. They had left the hospital and were walking along the street, which still had a fair bit of pedestrian traffic.

"All right," said Kunal, a large grin on his face. "He woke up briefly and went back to sleep. But he's going to be fine, just fine."

The BEST Bus jerked to a halt a short distance away from the *chawl*. Kunal and Nikhil jumped off. The road was almost deserted. A cat scurried across the street, chased by a rat almost as large as itself. Cars whizzed past now and then. In the distance a drunk belted out a Bollywood song at the top of his voice. The rest of Bombay slept.

"So, he'll be all right?" said Nikhil. "You're sure?"

Kunal nodded. "He'll pull through." *He has to.*

"We should have told the other *dabbawallas*, especially

Hari," said Nikhil. "They'll all be wondering about Vinayak when he does not show up tomorrow."

"There wasn't any time," said Kunal. "No point alarming them tonight. We'll tell them first thing in the morning. It's not like they can visit, nor can they do anything right now."

A slight figure stood by the *chawl*'s entrance, keeping to the shadows.

Nikhil nudged Kunal. "Who do you think that is?"

As they drew nearer, Kunal realized it was a woman. His pulse raced. It could only be one person. Should he dare hope she'd come, even though she'd refused to give out her number?

He quickened his step. As soon as they came closer, the woman started walking in the opposite direction. Kunal's heart sank. If it was his mother, she wouldn't be walking away. His stomach clenched and he tried to push her out of his mind. His thoughts flew to Vinayak again, lying alone in the hospital, tethered to a machine by all those tubes and wires. Had his talk with Vinayak helped? He decided that it had. Vinayak had looked very peaceful when he had closed his eyes.

"Look, she's coming back," said Nikhil, softly.

Sure enough, the woman had turned around as soon as she reached the end of the sidewalk. She approached them once again. Kunal stared at her. He'd already decided it couldn't be Anahita, but then, why did his heart say differently? Why was it beating at triple speed?

Nikhil nudged Kunal again. "Do you think ...," he said softly, "do you really think it could be her? She did say she was coming to see you soon."

"There's only one way to find out," said Kunal in a strangled whisper.

The woman hesitated for a moment, then walked purposefully towards them. Kunal marched towards her and waited under the streetlight.

The woman stepped into the pool of light and looked at Kunal. He met her gaze. She was pretty. And very nervous — eyes darting all around her, as if the shadows held hidden dangers. And in that instant he knew.

"Can you ...," she said in a husky voice. She stopped, cleared her throat. "Can you tell me ...," she spoke once again, her eyes fixed on Kunal.

"Madam," said Nikhil. "We can't stand here all night waiting for you to tell us what you want. Either ask or be on your way. We've had a really long day."

Kunal stared at the upturned nose, the fair complexion, and the full lips. Her eyes hadn't shifted from his face, even when Nikhil had been speaking, and he knew she had recognized him too. His heartbeat slowed, reverberating through him like the aftermath of a massive earthquake as he waited for her question.

Say something, he thought. *Say what I've waited twelve years to hear*. The thudding of his heart was loud in his ears and he willed it to soften. He didn't want to miss a word.

She said nothing.

At this moment he would have settled for a "Sorry."

"Can you tell me the way to Andheri Station, please?" she said, finally. Her voice was soft, shaky. Her eyes were rocksteady on Kunal's face.

Kunal's lungs were bursting and he realized he'd been holding his breath. He exhaled slowly and continued staring at her, unable to believe his ears. There were many first words he'd imagined exchanging with her. These did not fit in anywhere.

"It's that way," said Kunal. His throat was incredibly dry as he pointed out the route.

The woman started when he spoke. "Thank you," she said after a moment. "Thank you so very much."

She couldn't tear her eyes away from Kunal, nor could he look away, in spite of what she should have said and hadn't. For a moment it seemed as if the rest of Bombay had faded away and they were alone on that deserted street, immersed in light. Her face crumpled, as if she was in severe pain. She took a step back and the shadows claimed her again. She hurried past him, almost running now. Kunal watched her go, surprised that he had no desire to stop her. She looked back, saw him watching her, turned around, and hurried away.

"Very weird," said Nikhil, tapping his head. "It couldn't have been your mother."

They crossed the courtyard and climbed the steps in silence. Nikhil stopped on the second floor. Kunal continued up to the third floor, each step taking every ounce of will power. The shadows and darkness seemed to be dragging him down.

"Good night," Nikhil called out.

"Good night," replied Kunal, with some effort.

"Hey, Kunal!"

"Yes?"

"We completely forgot the main reason I came to see you this evening. Do you want to see your mother tomorrow? We can go after you've visited Vinayak and I've delivered the tiffins."

Kunal gripped the banister. His mother's face swam before his eyes, crumpled with pain yet, strangely, devoid of love. He remembered the deep satisfaction in Vinayak's when Kunal had accepted his offer to stay.

"You fallen asleep on the stairs or something?" said Nikhil. "Don't you want to see your family?"

"No," said Kunal. "I already have a family."

Glossary

Ahura Mazda: Avestan language for the divinity exalted by Zoroaster. In the Avesta, *Ahura Mazda* is the highest object of worship.

Aloo-Puri: Seasoned spicy potatoes served with fried bread.

Amitabh Bachchan: Famous Bollywood actor renowned for his daredevil stunts.

Anda Bhurji: Scrambled eggs, Indian style.

Ashem Vohu: One of two very important prayers in Zoroastrianism. The *Ashem Vohu*, after the *Ahunavar*, is considered one of the basic, yet most meaningful and powerful, mantras in the religion.

Baida Roti: *Roti* (or *chapati*) dipped in seasoned egg and cooked on a flat skillet.

Batata-Wadas: Seasoned boiled potatoes, dipped in chickpea batter and deep-fried.

Beedi: Homemade cigarette made with a dried leaf and filled with tobacco.

BEST bus: Brihanmumbai Electric Supply and Transport: Government organization that runs the public transport system.

Bhajiyas: Fried Indian snack that can be made with your choice of vegetable, such as cauliflower, onion, spinach, or potato.

Bhel: Also called *bhelpuri*, it is a puffed rice dish with potatoes and a tangy tamarind sauce. It is a type of *chaat* or small plates of savoury snacks, particularly identified with the beaches of Mumbai (Bombay), such as Chowpatty.

Bollywood: The film industry of Bombay, named in a similar fashion as Hollywood.

Chai: Hindi word for tea.

Chapatis: Type of unleavened flatbread from India.

Chawl: A type of building found in India. They are often four to five storeys high with about ten to twenty tenements, referred to as *kholis* (literally meaning room) on each floor. A usual tenement in a *chawl* consists of one all-purpose room that functions both as a living and sleeping space, and a kitchen that also serves as a dining room.

Chutiye: Slang for idiot. (Considered crude.)

Dabba: Box, or in this case, a tiffin.

Dabbawalla: A *dabbawalla* (literally, box person), also spelled *dabbawala* or *dabbawallah*, is a person in Mumbai (Bombay) who is employed in a unique service industry whose primary business is collecting the freshly cooked food in lunchboxes from the residences of the office workers (mostly in the suburbs), delivering it to their respective workplaces and returning back the empty boxes by using various modes of transport.

Dal-roti: Lentils and bread (*roti* is another word for *chapati*).

Dhaba: In India and Pakistan, highways are dotted with local restaurants popularly known as *dhaba*s (singular: *dhaba*). They generally serve local cuisine, and also serve as truck stops.

Dhoti-kurta: *Dhoti* is a traditional men's garment in India. It is a rectangular piece of unstitched cloth, usually around seven yards long, wrapped around the waist and the legs, and knotted at the waist. *Kurta* is a loose shirt falling either just above or somewhere below the knees of the wearer, and is worn by both men and women.

Faltu-giri: Rubbish or nonsense (in Hindi).

Flyover: An overpass.

Gadhera: Donkey.

Gandu: Crude slang for idiot.

Holi: Indian festival of colours.

Jaldi: Hindi word for quick.

Jalebis: Indian fried sweets, made by deep-frying batter in a kind of pretzel shape then soaked in syrup.

Jhootha: Lies in Hindi.

Junglee: Barbarian in Hindi.

Kasam se: I swear in Hindi.

Kheema Bun: A bun filled with savoury minced meat.

Kohl: A mixture of soot and other ingredients used predominantly by women in the Middle East, Africa, and South Asia to darken the eyelids and as mascara for the eyelashes.

Maharashtrian: An ethno-linguistic group of Hindu people from Maharashtra, India, speaking Marathi language.

Maska Pao: Bread and butter.

Memsahib: The way to address a woman with respect.

Paan or Meetha pan: South, East and Southeast Asian tradition that consists of chewing betel leaf (piper betle) combined with the areca nut. There are many regional variations. *Paan* is chewed as a palate cleanser and a breath freshener.

Pallu: The end of the *saree*, normally worn draped over the shoulder.

Panchgani: Is a town with a municipal council in Satara district in Mahashtra, India. Scenic Panchgani was discovered by the British during the British Raj as a summer resort.

Paratha: It is one of the most popular unleavened flatbreads in Indian cuisine and is made by pan-frying whole wheat flour on a griddle. The *paratha* dough usually contains ghee or cooking oil, which is also layered on the freshly prepared *paratha*. *Parathas* are usually stuffed with vegetables, such as boiled potatoes, radishes or cauliflower, and/or *paneer* (South Asian cheese).

Pehlwan: Big guy.

Phenyl: A brand of antiseptic floor cleaner available in India.

Raita: Yogurt thinned with water and with onions

and tomatoes added. Normally eaten with biryani to cut its spiciness.

Saala Paagal: Madman in Hindi.

Sambar: A vegetable stew or chowder based on a broth made with tamarind and *toovar dal* (a type of lentil). *Sambar* is very popular in southern regions of India, especially Andhra Pradesh, Karnataka, Kerala, and Tamil Nadu.

Samosa: Generally consists of a fried or baked triangular or half-moon-shaped pastry shell with a savoury filling of spiced potatoes, onion, peas, coriander, minced meat, or sometimes fresh *paneer*. Non-vegetarian *samosas* may substitute fillings of minced meat or fish. The size and shape of a *samosa* as well as the consistency of the pastry used can vary considerably, although it is mostly triangular.

Saree: A *saree* or *sari* is a garment worn by women in the Indian Subcontinent. A *saree* is a strip of unstitched cloth ranging from four to nine metres in length that is draped over the body in various styles. The most common style is for the *saree* to be wrapped around the waist, with one end then draped over the shoulder, baring the midriff.

Shabaash: Hindi word used to praise someone.

Tetrapods: Three-sided stones made of concrete to shore up the coastline of the reclaimed land along the Arabian Sea in Mumbai (Bombay).

Theek Hai: Okay in Hindi.

Yaar: Friend or pal in Hindi

Acknowledgements

You might as well get some popcorn now, sit back, and relax. Ready? Here goes ... I'd like to thank my friends and family in India for their help in getting the necessary footage of the *dabbawallas*, and Bombay in general. Special thanks to Kersi, Dolly and Nergish Irani, Hosi and Mani Billimoria, Khursheed Kanga, Naveen, Zubeen and Nafeesa Mehrotra, Shamin, Abuzer and Fouziya Indorewalla. Hugs to my family here, who continue to support and encourage me; Mom, Rahul, Aftab, Coby, Mazarine, Aziz, Zenia, Rayhan, Vicky and Dave. A heartfelt thank you to The Humber School for Writers, where this book first began its long journey, and to my brilliant mentor Tim Wynne-Jones, who steered me in the right direction, gently but firmly. Those few months were truly memorable!

Huge thanks to the Toronto Arts Council for their generous support of this project. Many thanks to my talented web designers, Vladimir Drizhepolov and Mike Cirillo, who have done such a fabulous job with my website and book trailers. And finally, a sincere thank you to my wonderful editor, Barry Jowett, who continues to believe in me, to my publisher Marc Côté and his wonderful team at Dancing Cat Books, Bryan Ibeas and Meryl Howsam, and to Gail Winskill for her insightful comments to make this a better book. I'd also like to thank my UK editors, Sarah Odedina and Jenny Jacoby, and everyone else at Hot Key Books for their tremendous support and enthusiasm. Though I'm almost out of creative ways to say thank you, I will say one last *shukriya* to all my readers. There would be no me, without you!

Mahtab Narsimhan

Mahtab was born in Mumbai, India, but at the time she grew up there it was called Bombay and always will be, in her mind. As a child, though not overly shy, she wasn't too enterprising or ambitious. She will forever be thankful to her mother, who pushed her to try out new things. Mahtab has always been an avid reader, and her childhood summers were filled with books, more books and sunshine. Mahtab is a Persian name meaning moonlight. She never really appreciated its beauty until recently and now that she does, all her books have some description of moonlight in each of them. So, that's her sharing her little secret!

Mahtab emigrated to Canada in 1997. Her first novel, THE THIRD EYE, took four years and twenty rewrites before making it to publication. It went on to win the Silver Birch Award in 2009. Mahtab lives in Toronto with her husband, Rahul, son, Aftab and her golden retriever, Coby. She continues to write, inspired by life, love and the desire to make sense of the world through stories.

Follow Mahtab at www.mahtabnarsimhan.com or on Twitter: @MahtabNarsimhan